USA TODAY bestselling author **Natalie Anderson** writes emotional contemporary romance full of sparkling banter, sizzling heat and uplifting endings—perfect for readers who love to escape with empowered heroines and arrogant alphas who are too sexy for their own good. When not writing, you'll find her wrangling her four children, three cats, two goldfish and one dog…and snuggled in a heap on the sofa with her husband at the end of the day. Follow her at natalie-anderson.com.

REVEALING HER NINE-MONTH SECRET

NATALIE ANDERSON

MILLS & BOON

First published in Great Britain 2022
by Mills & Boon, an imprint of HarperCollins*Publishers* Ltd,
1 London Bridge Street, London, SE1 9GF

www.harpercollins.co.uk

HarperCollins*Publishers*
1st Floor, Watermarque Building,
Ringsend Road, Dublin 4, Ireland

Large Print edition 2022

07/22

MIX
Paper from
responsible sources
FSC **C007454**

This book is produced from independently certified
FSC™ paper to ensure responsible forest management.
For more information visit www.harpercollins.co.uk/green.

Printed and Bound in the UK using 100% Renewable
Electricity at CPI Group (UK) Ltd, Croydon, CR0 4YY

For my Cheesy Crafts Crew.

You're the best bunch of witchy, wool-magic women…

Thanks for letting this lefty bring nothing but the cheese!

CHAPTER ONE

HOPE HADN'T *QUITE* DIED. Carrie Barrett glanced again at the door. A blind date with her workmate's cousin. Agreeing had been a terrible people-pleaser moment—second only to doing that reading at her sister's wedding. Since that horror fest she'd been trying to train herself out of the habit. But today she'd not just wanted to agree to a favour for someone else, she'd wanted to fit in. She'd even wanted to meet someone new.

It was a full year since she'd been jilted. Six months since she'd travelled from her home to the other side of the world. It was time to at least try and have some *fun*. But her date was late and a lifetime of punctuality meant Carrie was now sitting in a not-quite-fitted summer dress that wasn't even hers, conspicuously alone in the rooftop restaurant of the plushest waterfront hotel in Auckland, New Zealand.

At least she could avoid the waiter's enquiring looks by admiring the gleaming super yachts moored in the marina. The Waitematā harbour was especially stunning at sunset. But, despite the postcard perfection, she couldn't help glancing back to the door as more people arrived.

Please show up. It would be so great if someone would just show up. Just this once.

Her stomach somersaulted as a man walked in just as she willed it. Impressive height. Broad shoulders. Brilliant eyes—their focus landed directly on her. Just for a second.

It wasn't him, of course. Her date would be wearing a red jacket. This guy was entirely in black and the hold of his head, his all-encompassing gaze and his wholly confident stance sealed his command of the room. His arrival electrified everyone. They all turned, immediately straightening, eyes brightening, literally lip-licking.

Carrie wasn't miraculously immune. Goose bumps shimmied over her skin. Allergic, right? He was high performance personified. She'd been around the type long enough to instantly recognise the aura. Doubtless he'd be ruthlessly driven. As were her law-partner parents and champion-athletics stars sisters. Worst of all, her ex-fiancé too. Carrie *intimately* understood that the fight for success at the highest level meant other things got sacrificed—time and attention always, people often and sometimes someone wanted to win so badly they *cheated*.

Despite knowing this, she wasn't repelled by the new arrival but as transfixed as everyone else. He was a pirate, plundering hearts with the sheer authority of his presence. Even the ultra-professional and discreet maître d' took half a second to recover.

A murmured word and a moment later, the man followed the restaurateur. Only one empty table separated hers from his—now the last empty table. Apparently he felt no discomfort going solo in such a convivial setting. Of course, if he wanted company, he only needed to toss a glance at anyone crowding that bar and he'd be accosted in seconds. But he obviously didn't want, because he chose to sit with his back to them.

Which meant he faced her. Which meant she now had to look anywhere but straight ahead because otherwise she'd be staring right at him. It was as if they were at the same table—stretched apart by only a little distance.

So awkward.

She wanted to surreptitiously slither away. Instead, she watched the door. A woman arrived and another couple of men. They all went to the bar. She drew a disappointed breath and her gaze inadvertently slid over *him* and stopped. Because, just like that, time ended. He was more than a pirate. He had the beauty of an angel and the tempting gleam of a devil. And he was taking in far more than the colour of her hair.

Her cheeks heated as his gaze slowly swept over her features. Utterly fanciful thoughts filled her head. And, worse, her body actually reacted— heating as sensation zinged along her veins, tightening, *softening*. Shocking. Super-embarrassing. Also unstoppable.

The spell was only broken by the arrival of the maître d' at the man's shoulder. Her devilish pirate-angel angled his head to listen to the man but didn't take his eyes off her. But the interruption recalled her brain from its whimsical, sensual flight.

So, so awkward. Had he seen her reaction? Read her mind? But something had started unfurling inside and it couldn't be stopped. He said something in a low voice, and the maître d's eyes widened, but he nodded. Of course. Because this man got what he wanted. Every. Time.

But he wouldn't want *her*. She was way too ordinary. Like attracted like—superstars bonded with other superstars and that was as it should be.

Because the less bright got burned to bits when they got too close to stars like him.

'Would madam like to order or wait a while longer for her guest?'

The maître d's question mortified her. She'd been stood up. And she'd not ordered yet because this restaurant was *not* travelling-temp budget-friendly. But a random hit of pride made her refuse to walk out in front of the guy who had it all. The one who was still watching her. There'd be no slithering out without him noticing because he'd *already* noticed. For once, for this worst of moments, she was *not* invisible.

She wasn't his type. But Massimo Donati-Wells listened to the conversation between the maître d' and the strawberry blonde at the opposite table anyway. He'd already succumbed to the inexplicable urge to instruct the man not to allow anyone to be seated at the table between him and the petite woman with the pouting lips and soft-looking skin. He'd spotted her when he'd walked in and deliberately sat with his back to the rest of the room. She'd noticed him and, while that was hardly unusual, his shockingly instant response to her hyper-aware stare?

Very, *very* physical. It wasn't unwelcome. It

had been a long few days, and after the satisfaction of securing his latest contract a reward wouldn't go astray. So he sat back and didn't try to stop the current flowing. The electricity that had arced the moment he'd locked eyes with her had an addictive burst.

Her attention again flickered to the door over his shoulder. She was waiting for someone. A date? His muscles tensed. Foolish date for being late. Her phone pinged. Massimo unashamedly watched her read the message. She blinked rapidly and her mouth compressed.

'Actually, I will order something, please.' She called the maître d' back.

Pink-cheeked, the blue-eyed princess was clearly trying not to run. She was scraping together *pride*. Good for her.

'Um…' She didn't bother to scan the menu. 'A pina colada, please.'

He bit the inside of his cheek so he didn't smile. The beach cocktail classic wasn't even on the menu at this bar. It was known for its champagne selection. But the maître d' was too professional even to blink.

'Of course.'

She *really* wasn't his type. Too fresh. Too soft. The sort that blushed and probably dreamed of one true love. He selected the sort who played quick and never expected him to stay. The street-wise sort who were the same as him. But something kept him staring. Not just her smooth skin and soft curves, but the defiant courage shimmering in her sapphire eyes—and the vulnerability that underpinned it.

She shouldn't have been stood up. His ribs tightened, making his heart beat more forcefully against the constraints while his imagination slipped its chain and plotted just what she *should* be getting tonight. Touch. Definitely touch. The kind of touch to make her smile, sparkle, *scream.*

And he wanted her to look back at him so he'd feel that jolt of electricity again.

'Mind if I join you?' He called across the slight distance, shocking himself with his inability to resist temptation. 'My guest cancelled on me last minute.'

He'd wanted to dine alone. He'd had people seeking his pleasure and approval all day. This was supposed to have been an evening of peace before flying home tomorrow. And the strawberry-blonde sweetheart wasn't stupid. She pointedly glanced at the single place-setting at his table. Yeah, he'd just lied to her, and she knew it.

'Just a drink until your guest arrives…' he murmured, not used to having to ask anyone a second time.

In her heart-shaped face her smile twisted. 'He's not coming.' She didn't even try to lie.

'Then he's an idiot.' Massimo stood and moved seats before she could say anything more. 'I'm hungry,' he said equably. 'Are you?'

For a second he wondered if she was about to refuse. If he'd misread the arc of attraction that had bewitched him moments ago. If his customary boldness was too much for her. She was, after all, too soft.

But her chin lifted. 'I'm not sure. I can't actually think right now.'

The hit of honesty amused him. 'Let's find out.'

He glanced to his side and the maître d' materialised as if by magic. Massimo murmured his order.

'They serve tapas,' he explained after the man hurried away. 'I ordered some of everything.'

She assessed him with the clearest, bluest eyes he'd ever looked into and, despite the sizzling energy, there wasn't exactly approval shining in them.

'Everything? You must be hungry,' she said, sharpness edging her tone. 'You didn't want some big, juicy steak with a rich sauce and all the trimmings?'

A hint of challenge, of censure. She probably thought him a jerk and maybe he was. But there was another jolt of fire. Massimo wanted more because it warmed him in a way he hadn't felt in an age.

'Sampling lots of things is more fun than being stuck with only the one dish, don't you think?' He played up the arrogance she clearly read in him.

Suspicion firmed in her eyes. 'You mean you like to try *all* the different meats available on the charcuterie board?'

Her tart riposte burned in the best way. 'Absolutely. A nibble here, a nibble there. Sometimes, however,' he acknowledged swiftly, 'It's nice enough just to look.'

Because *she* probably shouldn't be on the board. He'd devour her and, despite her little push-back, he wasn't sure she'd handle it.

'Just looking leaves *you* satisfied?' she queried, disbelief audible. 'Your appetite is fully assuaged by little more than a glance?'

His ribs tightened even more. 'I guess it depends. What about yours?'

She looked at him for a long moment. 'I'm

still developing my palate. There's a lot I haven't tried.'

A ball of heat exploded in his loins. Hadn't she? Did she *want* to?

'You're very used to getting your own way,' she added after a moment. 'Do you choose from the board before anyone else gets a chance?'

He smiled. 'You think I would do that?'

'You don't bat an eyelid when ordering absolutely everything on the menu, having walked into a place and taking a seat at a table as if it were your own…'

He saw the moment she realised and her mouth formed an 'O'. It was a very luscious mouth. Massimo's watered.

'*Is* it your own?' She gazed at him intently. 'This hotel?'

'I'm only an investor.' Massimo had made so much money, he spent his days finding things to invest in. Well, fighting off the people who came to him asking for his investment and advice. His private equity empire was renowned for identifying future successful entities, meaning he simply kept making more money. He was not going to lie—he liked it. He liked success, liked living on his own terms. He also liked seducing pretty women who knew the score. This woman didn't.

'Only,' she echoed. 'So you only invest in high-end luxury hotels?'

'Actually, I'm currently focussing on renewable energy projects.'

A hint of humour stole into those blue eyes. 'Oh, how worthy.' She nodded. 'Do you hope to create a more sustainable future for your children?'

He stared back at her, appreciating the totally passive-aggressive niggle. No one had dared deal to him in a long while and he badly wanted to strike back with something inflammatory to provoke a reaction from her. The judgement got beneath his skin. 'Actually,' he said silkily. 'I have no intention of having children.'

'Naturally.' She smiled.

He shot her a look. 'Meaning?'

'Meaning, it is a truth universally acknowledged that every wealthy man feels a driving need to warn every female he meets that he's not in the market for either marriage or children.'

He looked at her, his mouth twitching. 'Quite.' He nodded firmly, appreciating her distortion of the famous literary line. 'So glad you readily understand my position.'

'I'm not in the market either, in case you were curious.' Her arrogance was completely faked.

He smirked. 'Which is why you're sitting here waiting for…?'

She eyed him severely but spoilt the look with an eventual smile. 'I was doing a friend a favour.'

'Oh, really? That's what you're going with?'

'It happens to be the truth.' She shrugged. 'But please, fear not, I'm only using you as a foil against public humiliation and for free food.'

'Okay,' he said. 'Glad we're able to be so frank. Equally, glad I'm able to oblige.'

'Indeed.'

'Who was he?' He was stupidly curious now. 'The idiot?'

'I don't even know. It was a set-up. I said yes for a friend but apparently the guy's been caught up at work.' The bitterness in her tone ran deep.

'Oh, workaholics.' He shook his head ruefully. 'Need to steer clear of those.'

A flash of disbelief widened her blue eyes, then her smile blossomed and a little laugh escaped. 'Indeed.'

That laugh was everything. He wanted more. He wanted that laugh in his *bed*.

'What about your date?' she asked.

'There wasn't one. I lied.' The pretence fell away and he was honest.

'Yes.' Her lashes lifted and those blue eyes

lanced through him. 'You've experience with that.'

'Doesn't everyone?' Now he was the one who couldn't keep a splinter of bitterness back. 'Both ways.'

'Apparently so.'

The connection between them suddenly flared and he felt a wave of empathy. He knew exactly how awful it was to be lied to.

A waiter arrived with her pina colada and a bottle of wine for him, severing the surprisingly solemn connection that had formed so suddenly.

'You're English,' he noted when the waiter was gone.

'You're Australian,' she countered with a smile.

Accents were the least of what they were noticing about each other.

'So we're both far from home, but you're the farthest. What brings you all the way to Auckland?' he asked.

He didn't want to know too much. He didn't want to get invested. He never did with women. He knew relationships ended up too intense. Too devastating. He just wanted to touch. But at the same time, for the first time, he wanted to know what it was that had made her look so alone.

'Adventure.' She sipped her drink. 'You?'

'Business. I'm heading back to Sydney first flight in the morning.'

Carrie looked into his eyes and saw the challenge lurking. He expected her to call him out on that and she wasn't able to resist. Because he was oh-so-not-very-smoothly letting her know he was here for only one more night. It was a form of arrogant weaponry, his arsenal against the threat of a woman wanting *more*.

Of course, this was a guy who *needed* defence, he was that attractive. And of course he *would* want children one day, once he met the right woman. *She* wasn't that woman—that was what had made her laugh. The ridiculousness of it. She was so far from his league, she'd been amused he'd felt the need to mention it.

'Gosh, what a shame you're not here for longer,' she said. 'I can't put my trap-you-into-marriage plan into action.'

He inclined his head. 'I find I'm devastated.'

'Indeed?' She stifled a laugh.

She usually didn't flirt so badly with anyone. She didn't flirt at all. But this was silly *easy*. That he'd commandeered the spare seat at her table and saved her from the indignity of dining alone, when all the staff knew she'd been waiting for a date. That he didn't seem to be able to take his eyes off her. That beneath that outrageous arrogance there was a core that called to something equally deep within her own soul.

'I'm Massimo.' He extended his hand across the table. 'Thank you for graciously allowing me to dine with you.'

'I'm Carrie. I'm not sure that you gave me much choice.' She put her hand in his.

A jolt sizzled along her skin at the contact. His fingers tightened.

'Allow me to correct that.' He looked across at her with total seriousness in his stunning eyes. 'Would you like me to stay or would you prefer to be left alone? I'll do whatever you wish.'

Whatever she wished? Carrie's breath vanished. Palm to palm, feeling that sizzle up her arm, she never wanted him to let go.

Any anxiety was vanquished by his touch and the vibrancy of his green eyes. Richly emphasised by lush lashes, the colour was striking enough from a distance. Up close, it was mesmerising. No wonder he needed to warn women away.

But, while he was confident, there was more to him than money-man arrogance. More depth, more humanity than the stereotype she'd pinned on him. No caricature, he was flesh and blood, hot and *hurt*. Quite how she knew that, she wasn't sure. But she was certain of its truth. In this one moment, Massimo needed her as much as she needed him. Just for company at dinner.

'You can stay,' she said flatly.

'Thank you.'

Massimo released her hand as the maître d' approached, flanked by two waiters. All three carried wooden platters that they placed on the table. She diverted herself from the shocking intensity of her feelings by taking in the vast array. There was fresh oysters, each kept cool in its open shell with a spoonful of champagne granita. There was a dish of baked brie, as well as a trinity of boards—cheese, charcuterie and chocolate.

'There's a lot of food here,' she said.

'We can take our time.' He shrugged. 'But is there something to tempt that elusive appetite of yours?'

She took in the other offerings. Olives. Ceviche. Vegan tartlets and tempura vegetables. Even salted potato crisps. There was something to tempt almost anyone.

'What are you doing in Auckland, Carrie?' Massimo couldn't resist the urge to find out more about her. He wanted to know everything.

'Working as a temp,' she said. 'Office administrator. I plan to head somewhere warmer soon.'

'Sydney?' he immediately suggested with a smile.

'Too big.' She dismissed it just as instantly with a laugh. 'I want smaller and more isolated.'

He glanced at her cocktail. 'Fiji? The Cook Islands?'

She nodded, her enthusiasm building. 'Paradise.'

His brows lifted. 'You think?'

'Don't you?'

The topic was light and breezy and he didn't quite believe everything she was saying. But then, he didn't believe everything anyone said.

'An island holiday wouldn't be paradise, it would be boring,' he said blandly.

'Boring?' She laughed. 'You disappoint. I thought you'd have a better imagination.'

Massimo's imagination was firing up most unhelpfully right now. 'How would you fill your days?'

'A walk early in the morning. Then a swim. Fresh fruit to awaken the palate…'

Fresh fruit and awakenings of palate made him laugh. 'You've thought about this.'

'Often.' She nodded with perfect seriousness before stunning him with a wide smile.

'Are we talking meditation and yoga poses along the shoreline?' he teased. 'Shots for your social media?'

'Walking is meditative,' she agreed. 'But no socials. They don't keep one *present*. I would read. A book a day.'

'If it doesn't inform me on investments, then I'm not reading it,' he said blithely.

'No novels? No history? No philosophy?' She shot him a look as he shuddered theatrically. 'No *poetry*? Reading can inform your soul.'

'You assume I have a soul.'

'I do believe you're human,' she countered dryly. 'Therefore, have imagination. And I bet yours is good.' She cocked her head. 'So I don't believe you about the books.'

His gaze intensified on her. 'Why do you think I have a good imagination?'

'Because success takes more than brains and business acumen. It takes vision and creativity.'

'And you understand this…?'

'Because I've been around other successful people.'

He paused. The edge to her tone suggested she wasn't that thrilled to have known these successful people. She classed them as belonging to a group other than her. 'Yet you don't seem to want to stick around them. You want to escape to an isolated island.'

She stiffened. 'I'm not escaping. I'm enriching my life with *adventure*.'

'Are you?' He shook his head. 'Or are you enriching your life with someone *else's* dreams and adventures in their books?'

'So you're an adrenalin junkie rather than a beach-read, relaxation holiday sort, or—?' She suddenly broke off as she realised the even worse truth. 'No. I've got it wrong. You don't holiday at all.' She sat back and looked at him as if he were a lost cause. '*You're* a fully paid-up member of workaholics not-so-anonymous.'

'Well,' he drawled not-so-apologetically. 'The demands on my very expensive time are too great.'

'And of course you prioritise the demands that *pay* over those that are personal.' Bitterness underlined her scorn. 'What do you do exactly—spend your days deciding which exciting new companies you should invest your pots of gold into?'

'That's not far off the mark, actually.'

'And everyone wants to be your friend because

you A, have the gold, and B, can pick the winners?'

'Hence my wariness when it comes to women…' He shot her a smug glance.

Her laugh was reluctant. 'Yes, you're clearly such a wallflower. While I'm clearly a gold-digger.' She shook her head. 'Super-successful people make great personal sacrifices.'

'Now you think I don't have balance in my life?'

'I'm sure of it.'

He pressed his hand to his chest in mockery of being wounded. But, in truth, his heart was pounding too hard for comfort. 'Contrary to your judgement, I *do* know how to relax.' He leaned closer. 'But I can assure you, copious amounts of sand *aren't* part of a good time.'

'But there might be good sustainability projects in the islands for the future of those children you're not having.' She parodied his worthiness.

'Perhaps I should investigate.' He smiled. 'I like a challenge.'

'Reading on the beach all day *can* be a challenge,' she informed him with *faux* earnestness. 'The angle of the sun, ensuring you're not getting burned…' She shook her head at him sadly. 'But *you* can't get past the need to accumulate, to score that thrill—high risk and high reward, high speed, need to win at all costs…'

'There's nothing wrong with chasing the best rewards.' He shrugged. He'd make no apology for driving for success. It was how he'd survived. 'But you shouldn't read on the beach all day. You'll get sunburned.'

Her lips twisted in a little smile. 'I promise to cover up.'

Fierce heat hit him low down. 'People shouldn't make promises,' he muttered, trying to joke but failing. 'They tend not to keep them.'

Her blue gaze shone at him. Her voice was soft. 'Actually, on that we agree.'

That thread pulled, tugging him closer to her. It was moored to an elemental weight within him, something raw that he recognised she also had deep inside. Something sore.

'Here's to no promises, then,' he said quietly.

'No promises.' She lifted her glass, the bright cocktail at odds with the sombre note in her voice. 'No lies.'

How was it that one *look* had sparked madness to life? Carrie had turned into someone she didn't recognise—her awkwardness melted, she laughed easily and joked lightly. Yet humour barely hid the chemistry pushing them closer—

beneath the frothy flippancy, that killer electrical current pulsed with tempting, decadent danger.

With the grazing platters between them, there were no interruptions from the staff. After she'd finished her cocktail, Massimo leisurely filled her glass with the warming red wine at required intervals. There was no natural conclusion of each course, so time, that had ended the moment when she'd first enmeshed her gaze with his, now raced, spinning on an invisible loom. Long stretches disappeared between breath, look and teasing banter, soft, silly arguments that neither of them really meant yet weren't entirely untrue. Hours evaporated into the atmosphere, unrealised, unseen, so easily sucked away.

It was the clatter of crystal in the kitchen that brought her back to reality. Glancing around, Carrie realised they were the only two diners remaining. The staff had cleaned and put away everything from the other tables. Even the bar at the other end of the rooftop terrace was now quiet. Yet there was still food on their platters, still wine in their bottle. They'd barely begun. A glance at Massimo's expensive watch showed the hands well on the other side of midnight. She had work tomorrow. He had a flight home. This flirt would never lead to anything more.

It wouldn't have *anyway*—even if he'd lived in town. Massimo was way beyond her earthly plane, up in the stratosphere somewhere. Superstars didn't stick with mortals like her. She'd learned that the hard way. But that meant it didn't matter what she said or did right now. Because there was *only* now. It was stupidly easy to talk, tease him and say things she'd not normally mutter aloud. Growing up in a house of success stories, with people who couldn't understand why she didn't set her expectations higher, who didn't have time for dinner because they were too busy training, too busy pushing, and for whom spending time together wasn't a priority…it hadn't just been lonely. It had been hard.

Don't interrupt my focus... Don't be a fool...

And Massimo was one of them, wasn't he? A driven workaholic who prioritised performance over the personal. Carrie should have broken out in hives already. But she hadn't, because he wasn't working now. Now, humanity lurked in his eyes. Hot, hurt, lonely. Surely she was wrong? Surely this guy lacked nothing?

'I ought to get going,' she murmured.

She didn't want to. Beneath that easy fun, regardless of their differing lifestyle goals, they'd connected. It was just lust, right? They had stellar chemistry despite being so strikingly different. It was new to her. And shockingly powerful.

Massimo reluctantly nodded. He could suggest she come back for a drink. She would understand the implication…she would say yes and he could, would, win. But as much as he ached for it—because he ached for it so *unbearably*—he found this wasn't a game. Not tonight. This was imbued with something other than the usual quest of catch and release and short-lived, decadent hedonism. Oddly, this was more precious. He'd enjoyed simply talking to her. Talking frippery and teasing nonsense. Yet they'd both known something serious simmered underneath at the same time.

He was *not* taking advantage. She *wasn't* his type. She was not a carefree, experienced woman who understood someone like him. She'd been hurt—tonight was the least of it, he suspected. She was emotionally vulnerable, right? Which meant she was out of bounds. Because high emotion wasn't something he could manage.

Besides, the intensity of the driving urge to pull her close…the compelling need to brand her as his, somehow… That sharp ache wasn't just foreign, it was too strong. He would resist simply to prove he could. Because it was a near-run thing.

But he accompanied her in the lift down to the dark street, where a taxi waited to take her away. Carrie faced him, her old awkwardness filling her fast. 'Thank you for dinner,' she mumbled.

It sounded inadequate. Worse, she knew she sounded *forlorn*.

This *wasn't* a pick-up. He'd merely been amusing himself. He'd felt sorry for her and had been filling in time during a boring business-trip dinner. The ease with which they'd laughed was now lost in a jelly-like slop of mortification. She couldn't get out of here soon enough because otherwise she was going to do something stupid. But he reached out and took her hand and that electricity sparked again. He looked into her face but said nothing. For a second, he didn't seem able to move, as if he didn't want to let go of her hand.

But then he did.

She quickly climbed into the taxi. He leaned down to the open window, only it was too dark for her to read his expression.

'Bye, Carrie.' The stark thread in his voice pulled taut an answering thread within—like a leash tethering them at the very core. It tugged up temptation. But it was too late.

As he stepped back, the street light illuminated his face. The bleak, unbearable expression of loneliness shocked then echoed within her. It gave name to the seriousness that hadn't been absent but unacknowledged until now.

Desolation.

The taxi was already carrying her away. She twisted in her seat to keep her gaze on him, wanting to catch a glimmer of his lighter charm. Wanting to know she'd been mistaken. But the last impression she had of him was of pain.

For a few minutes she could hardly think and then slowly a sense greater than regret filled her. Urgently she leant forward to speak to the driver. 'Please, would you mind turning around?'

She would just drive by. He'd have gone back into the hotel. But, illuminated by the lights along the waterfront, was a tall, lone figure. Hands deep in his pockets, he faced the inky, almost invisible sea. He glanced round at the sound of the car. Then he glanced again. His gaze held and suddenly, swiftly, he walked over as it approached the kerb, ready to open the door as soon as it pulled up.

Wordlessly, he held out his hand to her.

CHAPTER TWO

HE DIDN'T LET go of her hand. In the darkness it was still impossible to read his expression. But his grip tightened, he tugged her closer and she *knew*. Astonishing as it was, he wanted her.

'You came back.' His husky whisper was almost wonderstruck.

'I didn't want tonight to be over,' she confessed.

'I'm...' He cupped her face and released a ragged breath. 'My mind has failed. I just want to kiss you.'

'Oh.' She breathed a ragged breath of her own at the sizzling jolt from the touch, intent and that hint of amazement. A beat of delight of her own. 'Good.'

That sizzling current of electricity hummed higher and louder. She didn't want to shut it off. She leaned closer, already addicted to the intimate tease of his fingers on the side of her neck. A cascade of sensations shimmered down her body as his touch lit her deepest, darkest places. She wanted this. She wanted *more*.

His lips hit hers. Finally. It was like coming home and shooting for the moon at the same time—perfect and fierce. That current of energy arced and she closed her eyes at the blinding white brilliance of starburst and pleasure. His mouth was soft and firm, taking and giving, and she opened instantly, leaning, learning, *aching*. His hands were everywhere, pressing her closer as his kiss deepened. It was not plundering but perfect. The demanding pressure of his body pressed full length against hers heated her so much more than physically and she grabbed him hard. Combustion was so close. She was hot and breathless in seconds. There was only one way this could go.

He tore his lips from hers, barely able to breathe. 'Come with me.'

'Yes.'

He didn't let go of her hand. He walked her along the marina, towards the water. Towards the dark. He stopped at far end of the wooden walkway and she stared at the yacht gleaming in the silvery moonlight.

'Are you staying on *that*?' she asked. 'Not the hotel?'

His smile flashed. He really was a pirate. 'That okay or do you get seasick?'

'Well, we're not actually going anywhere, are we?'

'We're definitely going somewhere,' he muttered and led her up the gangway. He placed his free hand on a small flat screen, and after a faint whirring sound the door lock clicked.

'Very high-tech.' She breathed, paying attention and yet not. She needed to touch him again and it was crazy.

'It's not mine,' he said as the door slid open and he led her inside.

'I bet you're an investor,' she teased.

He turned that stunning smile on her. Peripherally she absorbed the stunning interior of the yacht but, honestly, she couldn't drag her attention from him.

'Would you like a drink?' he offered but completely ignored the sparkling bar behind him. Keeping her hand tightly in his, he stepped into her space and placed his other hand on her waist before she could even think of an answer.

That jolt again. Heart racing, blood zinging, she spread her hand back on his chest, glad that he too seemed as eager as she was for this contact. His heat burned through his black shirt. He was real, not a fantasy of her wildest dreams. This *wasn't* a dream and suddenly she was driven to be honest.

He needed to know—not only because it would be unfair not to tell him, but because instinctively she knew he'd accommodate her wishes.

'I've never done this before,' she said huskily. 'Any of this.'

His eyes widened and he cocked his head. *'Any?'*

Her mouth dried, but somehow she still wasn't scared. It was still okay to tell him her secret. 'Not any. None. *Nada.*'

His heart kicked beneath her fingers. 'Then perhaps we shouldn't…'

Verbally he was leaving it up to her, but she read the intensity in his eyes and felt that current flowing back and forth between them. The electrical impulse made her heart pound in sync with his. She'd never experienced anything like that kiss and perhaps never would again. Which was why there was no hesitation. 'But perhaps we should.'

His pulse picked up, even as he nodded. 'What if anything and everything is on offer?' he asked huskily, still careful with her. 'What if you get to pick and choose? You can have as little as you like, or you can have the lot. And you can change your mind any time.'

Desire unravelled at the prospect of him putting himself forward so completely for *her* pleasure. Suddenly she struggled to breathe at all. 'That doesn't seem fair. What about what you want?'

A smile stole into his heated gaze. 'I'm confident you'll choose well.'

Oh? She wrinkled her nose. 'Because that's been your experience?'

'No,' he said. 'Because chemistry like this can't be contained.'

His sudden solemn note surprised her. 'Isn't it always like this?'

He lifted his hand, softly torturing that intensely sensitive skin on her neck again. 'Has it been like this for you before?'

'No, but—'

'Me neither.'

That was pure charm, wasn't it?

But he held her hip and gently pressed against her so she felt the length of him against her belly. His very hard length. 'This part of me can't lie.'

She shook her head. 'That's a physical response to...'

He leaned closer, crushing her hand against his chest. His heart raced the gallop of hers. 'Chemistry this strong is scary.'

She gazed up into his intense green eyes. 'Scary?'

His grip on her hip tightened. 'I don't want to let you down. You were meant to meet someone else tonight.'

'I've never even spoken to him. Maybe I was meant to meet you instead. Maybe this is the universe granting me one special night. I mean, you're leaving in the morning. You're not in the marriage market. Most importantly, you're not my type.'

He smiled but the expression in his eyes was still serious. 'No, I'm not.'

Yet something in him called to something true deep within her and she knew he felt the same. They shared a commonality. She didn't know what, or why, but somehow she knew there was *recognition*. And because of that a boldness she'd never imagined feeling swept over her. She was going to take this moment because, if she didn't, she'd always regret it.

'You don't need to protect me,' she said softly. 'You need to please me.'

'You deserve much more than one special night,' he said.

Didn't everyone? Didn't he? But, the fact was, life didn't work that way. It wasn't fair. Carrie knew that.

'There's only *now*,' she said. 'That's all there ever is.'

She'd come back to him. He knew it had taken a boldness she didn't usually feel—certainly not if she'd never done this before. Whoever had made her doubt herself ought to be shot, and that guy who'd let her down tonight was a fool. But Massimo had never been more grateful. Because, while she wasn't his type, she was the fantasy he'd never dared dream of and he'd never wanted a woman as much. Damn it if he didn't admire her courage. If he wasn't amused by the way she talked back to him. If he wasn't humbled by her return.

So he moved. Fast. Scooping her into his arms, he strode to the master bedroom and set her down before desperately activating the electronics. She chuckled as the vast curtains closed and the room was softly lit. Then the world was shut out and there was only the two of them, and he was pleasing her if it was the last thing he'd ever do.

Because she'd come back. She was his. Just for tonight. And now he would take his time. She stood still as he walked towards her. Nerves and anticipation were apparent in her blue eyes, but there was certainty too—and lush, sensual appreciation as he unfastened the buttons of his shirt. He didn't know how she'd got to this night, never having had sex before. But he was shockingly pleased he now got to be the one to show her how. And why.

She was made for pleasure. He loved the lift of her chin as she met him, the warm softness of her willing, pliant body. He kissed her, consumed in the fire in seconds, desperately trying to slow down but failing. His hands worked, racing ahead of his intentions. The dress slid from her shoulders into a satiny puddle on the floor and for a split-second all he could do was stare.

'You're sensational,' he rasped. He cupped her breasts in his hands, loving the way they spilled over the top of her simple satin bra. He felt her self-conscious shiver and glanced up to tease her. 'Not going to argue with me?'

'I've decided to believe your flattery. It's my fantasy night.'

'It's not flattery.' Suddenly he didn't want to pretend this was nothing. He didn't want her to either. He wanted her to believe him. And he wanted her to be *sure* of what she was doing. 'And it's not a fantasy. Don't forget this is *real*.'

Overwhelmingly real, and the intensity still scared him if he stopped to consider it. So he didn't stop. She was so hungry for his kisses, he couldn't.

She pressed against him, her softness moulding to his hardness, filling the gaps, heating him in places and in ways he'd not known needed warming. As she leaned into his lush, slow kisses he felt a deepening intimacy, a deepening connection that he'd not anticipated. His control of the situation rapidly slid away from him. He lifted her to the bed and could barely keep his hands steady enough to gently remove her bra and matching navy panties.

'You've got no idea how badly I want you.' He all but ripped the rest of his clothes off. 'I'm trying really hard to slow down.'

Because he wanted this to be so good for her. Trouble was, his hunger was almost out of control, and the look in her eyes as she stared at his bared body wasn't helping.

Shock. Appreciation. Anticipation. He knew how she felt. He wanted to taste *all* of her, not just zero in on the ripest treasures like some sex-starved youth. He wanted to trace the soft skin at the backs of her knees and gently press his teeth to test the delicate flesh of her inner thighs. Damn it, yes, he just wanted to lick her in the most intimate part of all, to taste and tease until she was totally ripe and ready for the rest of him. And she didn't help his control. Instead she encouraged him to race, instinctively parting her legs, circling her hips, compelling him closer to that very part until he couldn't resist discovering all her sweet secrets.

Growling in feral pleasure, he discovered how slippery and how hot she was. Her sighs drove him out of his mind. Goose bumps rippled over his skin as the effort to delay pleasure almost broke him. He'd wanted to go slow, to impress with finesse. But there was no bloody finesse. There was only hunger in his exploration and an incredible, unexpected joy.

Because she was with him at every step. Having his hands on her, having her spread before him, made him feel like the wealthiest man in the world, rich in bountiful softness and heat, and that snug, secret part that he was first to explore. He was going to have *all* of her, like the selfish glutton he was.

The sight of her pleasure, the sounds as she released the shackles of shyness, undid him. Self-restraint obliterated, she grasped his hair and rocked her hips hard, utterly abandoned in her pursuit of the satisfaction she instinctively knew he could give. He knew it too. He'd recognised it the second he'd seen her sitting alone in that restaurant. Electricity and chemistry, the basic building blocks of life, that raw *want*, had smacked into both of them.

Carrie couldn't cope with the sensations piling over her. His grip was hard as he held her bucking hips so he could keep tormenting her with his tongue. He wouldn't let her escape. And she didn't want to, she just wanted the *peak*— the finish she knew he was holding just out of her reach. She relished the sight of him halfway down the massive bed, intently focused on teasing her swift response, craving it as much as she did. The game in his gaze had sparked her own playfulness, overpowering her initial shyness of such intimacy. Nothing felt more natural, easy, right and utterly *infuriating*.

'Don't stop,' she begged, arching again and again.

'Hmm?' He smiled up at her.

His enjoyment of her torment only turned her on more.

'Don't stop,' she repeated on her held breath.

But he did. His fingers ceased their deliciously wicked strumming. The teasing smile on his angelically, sinfully, beautiful face stirred a fire within her.

'Don't stop.' But it was an order that time.

His smoky green gaze was so full of wicked intent, it drove her wild. But she couldn't move as she watched him lower his mouth and sucked, his fingers and tongue striking up their fast play again. And, just like that, she lost herself.

'Don't stop. Don't stop. Don't stop.' She chanted the command, the plea, sobbing until she didn't even know what the words meant.

The last thing she saw before squeezing her eyes shut were the muscles rippling in his wide, bronzed shoulders and the wild burst of fire in his eyes. And she screamed as pleasure tumbled through her. Uncivil sensation. All emotion in her abandonment.

When she opened her eyes she saw his. The stunning green was now only the narrowest ring around the wide black pupils. Dark and dangerous. Utterly inviting. But he was watching, waiting. And he was wonderful.

'Don't stop now,' she said softly.

He swallowed hard. 'If you give me this, I can't give it back.'

'You're giving me something else in return. Something I get to keep.'

His lush lashes fluttered. 'What's that?'

'A perfect memory.'

'Perfect?' His eyebrows arched. 'Stop. I'll get performance anxiety.'

'You know it's already perfect!' She half-laughed, but it was true. 'I just want you.'

'I'm...' he drew in a breath '...honoured.'

He rummaged in the sleek drawer beside the bed. 'Hell, I hope...' He straightened, an almost boyish smile of relief on his face. 'Thank God.'

His hands shook as he tore open the square packet. She saw him breathing carefully as he rolled the condom down his rigid length. He glanced over at her and stifled a moan that sounded almost despairing. 'I want you so much, I'm afraid I might fail you.'

That *he* wanted *her* was mind-blowing in it-self, but she knew how desperately he wanted to *please* her. This heart-stopping man was no pi-rate. He had depth and, for all the playful banter and pretence, an honesty of intention that touched her far more than physically.

'I want you to take pleasure in me too,' she admitted. 'I think… I think it's impossible not to.' Because just one kiss had felt ridiculously good. Every touch since had been designed to send her insane. 'It's chemistry.'

He moved, bracing his entire length above her in a show of strength and muscled beauty. She couldn't help staring at his straining erection. That part of him looked magnificent. And big.

'Don't worry.' He nudged her thigh with his hand and gently strummed between her legs. 'I've got you so hot and slippery, I'll slide in.'

She gaped at his raw, sensual claim, but his smile widened as he pressed his finger into her.

'See?'

He turned her on even more, filling her with his fingers, pressing his thumb against her sensitive nub. She groaned and then his mouth was on hers. She strained, loving the sensations as he teased her, realising he was readying her for more. He kissed down her neck, inhaling her scent, gliding lips over her skin as if he couldn't get enough of her. She gasped as he pushed her close to that edge again. She wanted it. But she wanted it *all*. She wanted not just his hand, but his…

'Talk to me, Carrie,' he murmured, an intimate invitation.

Seriously?

'And say what?' She panted.

His soft laugh was more of a choke. She giggled too but she was shockingly desperate for him to hurry and claim all she'd offered.

'Is this a final consent question or something? Because I want it, okay? You're good to go. Full steam ahead.'

He laughed again. 'Oh, Carrie, you're good for my soul.'

'Your ego, you mean.' She had just enough breath to tease. 'You said you didn't have a soul.'

'Maybe I was wrong.'

She cupped the side of his face with her hand and smiled into his stunning eyes. 'Of course you were.'

He didn't just have soul. He had humour, heart and all the good human things, most especially generosity, and she trusted him utterly.

He pushed her legs wider, settling his hips between her slick thighs. The hard ridge of his erection pressed big and heavy, and she couldn't do anything other than look into his eyes. She couldn't even breathe. He didn't let go hold of her hand. They were palm to palm, chest to breast, hip to hip. He was taut, intense, and so deliciously careful as he slowly pushed against her, then into her.

'Just like that.' He groaned, his tension building as he watched her close. 'Okay?'

The eroticism of his possession…his body in hers, his fingers laced through hers… She shook, almost giddy with the intensity, pleasure literally shafting through her. She smiled at him. She couldn't not. She couldn't hold anything back.

His concentrated expression broke apart, his answering smile radiating. She breathed out. This was so much simpler than she'd ever imagined it would be. It was easy. And intimate—not in a scary way but a hot, funny, sweet way.

She wriggled, lifting her hips to meet the slow rhythm of his. 'Just like that?'

His assenting growl satisfied that deeply buried part of her. That yearning for recognition, for connection. But then he moved. And then it wasn't so funny, it wasn't so sweet. It was *scorching*. And she moved with him, unrestrained in the fierceness. Between the blinding flashes of her own erotic annihilation, she saw the moment that he caved beneath the unbearable need to release all he had left. She felt the final thrust of his powerful body, the rasping catch of his cry, the power he could no longer control. The force of pleasure flowed between them in an utterly unstoppable form.

And he didn't let go of her hand.

'I can't...' *Think.*

Words...what were they?

She was spent—she'd never felt as limp or as dazed. Yet warmth trickled through her. It was as if she had a new baseline temperature, as if her engine now ran on new fuel—bliss.

He lifted, shifting to lie beside her. But he pulled her into his arms, pressing her head to rest on his chest. His fingers skimmed across her back, his touch light, as if he knew how highly sensitised her skin still was. How raw her soul was. How it needed soothing touch. He traced down her arm, catching her fingers with his once more. And then...

He didn't let go of her hand.

CHAPTER THREE

FIJI. A SIX-MONTH CONTRACT. Visa and accommodation sorted. Sun. Sand. And, yes, *escape*. Carrie couldn't wait to fly out next week. It was going to be brilliant. Walking towards her temporary office job in central Auckland, she glimpsed the marina in the distance, filled with luxury boats. Her heart twisted but she steadied her wistfulness with her secret, often muttered, refrain—at least she'd had that one special night.

She had no regrets. *None*. It was done. And she was okay.

She'd not rung the number Massimo had left for her before heading to his flight that morning just over a month ago. Okay, in occasional weaker moments she'd mentally composed a few text messages, but she'd not let herself send them. It had been a perfect moment, but a *moment* was all it was, and would ever be. She wasn't spoiling it by asking for more only to have him eventually say no. Because that *would* have happened.

But, even though she knew that, her confidence

had lifted from the encounter. She'd asked for what she'd wanted once—with him—and she'd since asked again with something else. She'd applied for a job she'd never thought she'd actually get, figuring she had nothing to lose…and the result?

Fiji. A six-month contract. Visa and accommodation sorted.

All she needed now was to shake off the stomach upset that had plagued her these last few days. But as she passed the coffee stand outside her office she gagged so violently she knew she had to go home. She couldn't spread anything in the office and she needed to get well enough to travel next week.

She stopped at a pharmacy on her way home to get something to settle her stomach. 'Any chance you're pregnant?' the pharmacist asked quietly when she'd explained her symptoms.

'No chance.' Carrie laughed. There'd never been a chance in her life.

Uh…actually, there had.

Her smile faded as she suddenly remembered. In a millisecond, hot sweat slicked over her body and that nausea returned.

'Here, take a seat.' The pharmacist sent her a sympathetic smile. 'Breathe. It'll be okay.'

It wasn't okay. It wasn't possible—*surely*?

Carrie purchased the test the pharmacist fetched and got home as quickly as she could. She was so shaken up she had to read the instructions three times before they made sense. He'd used protection. He'd definitely used protection. She remembered his relief at finding some on that outrageously opulent boat. More moments from that night crowded her mind. Searing pleasure. The multiple times he'd made her scream with satisfaction. Then a rush of something else flooded her. Pure protectiveness.

Because the result….

Pregnant. Pregnant. Pregnant.

She lost hours muttering it in shock. Then performed the mental gymnastics of *what the hell was she going to do*? How was she going to tell him? How might he react? How she was going to cope? What were her parents going to say?

They were going to judge this as a failure, of course. And he was going to be appalled. This was so not in his plan.

But there was one positive certainty in her mind. She *wanted* this baby. She was having this baby. This miracle, this lapse of fate, was *hers*. And she would be and do everything she could for this child. Because this child deserved all the love in the world.

She needed to tell him in person, to *see* his reaction. But she couldn't fly to Australia and turn up on his doorstep. For one thing, she couldn't afford it. For another, she didn't know where he lived. She only had a number for him so, no matter what, she was going to have to call first.

Feeling sick all over again, she reached for her phone and checked the time. She'd lost most of the day in a haze of rumination and confusion, but it would be early afternoon in Sydney. That was assuming he was even in Sydney. Or that he'd even answer. But she had to try. A video call would work—so she would still see him—and that was what she'd do. Panicked choices flooded her mind and she moved before she could ruminate and end up uncertain of anything. She just had to act. Telling him was imperative.

Moments later, his face filled her phone screen. For a few seconds she could only stare—her heart had stopped…she couldn't breathe. It should have been impossible but those perfect angles of his face, and the bronzed skin that offset those stunningly vibrant green eyes that were now wide, were even more handsome.

'Carrie?' Pure astonishment sounded then he

glanced to the side of the screen. 'I need a moment.'

He muttered something unintelligible to someone unseen, then she heard a door close.

'This is a surprise. You—' He paused, frowning directly into the screen. 'Is everything okay?'

She hadn't expected to see him ever again and now she was. Her bursting heart pounded into her throat. How did she plan to tell him?

'I'm pregnant.'

For a second she thought the screen had frozen because he didn't even blink. But then she heard the audio.

'That's not possible.'

'Well, obviously it is,' she floundered. 'Because I'm pregnant.'

The screen hadn't frozen, because an awfully cold expression hardened his face. 'No. I used protection. You know I did.'

Yes. But…did she have to point out the obvious? 'Apparently protection doesn't always work.'

'No.' He repeated that damning, revealing, rejection. 'That's not been my experience to date.'

'And, as you know, I don't have any other experience to date.' Her grip on her emotions slipped. 'I'm telling you, I'm pregnant.'

'No.' Massimo stared, simply nonplussed. 'That's *not* possible.'

How had his day gone from fantastic to fatal in one split-second? She was a stranger to him now, growing paler by the second until she had a positively greenish tint, and it wasn't some filter on the phone. He couldn't comprehend what she was saying.

Pregnant? *No.*

His reaction was visceral, violent, an outright rejection because it *was* impossible. He wasn't having children. He'd *not* got her pregnant. He would never get a woman pregnant. Never take that risk. He'd used protection. Every time. So he didn't believe her. He couldn't.

This had to be something else. This had to be a trick. What was she planning? What was the point of this? For all their banter that night, had she played the innocent but actually been the player? Did she think she could take him for a ride?

'I did a test earlier today.' She sounded adamant. And angry.

He didn't believe her for a second. It was far too improbable. *Impossible.* A million questions flooded his mind. He shook his head. 'It's not possible.' People lied—all people, all the time. 'Do you take me for a fool?'

'A fool?' She stared at him as if he'd just grown horns and fangs. 'Don't you *believe* me?'

It hadn't occurred to Carrie that he wouldn't believe her. That he'd turn so cold. She'd not imagined he'd speak quite so harshly—not just judging her but *hating* her.

'Why don't you believe me?' This was worse than anything. Even worse than when her sister had revealed her betrayal. 'Should I get the test and prove it to you?'

'You're going to need several tests.'

Her jaw dropped. What did that even mean? A test to prove she was pregnant? A test to prove *he* was the father?

'How could you think I'd make this up? That I would lie to you?' She struggled to understand his thinking. 'I might have been the ultimate loser the night we met, but I'm not so desperate that I'd… I'd…' She couldn't even figure out what nefarious plan it was that he thought she was capable of.

'I'm…' He clenched his jaw.

'You're what?' Her anger billowed.

He lifted his chin. 'Very wealthy.'

She stared at him for another moment as her

shocked brain took an eternity to process what he was implying.

'You *jerk*.' Her mouth was so dry and her throat so tight, it was nigh impossible for sound actually to emerge. But just enough did. 'You think I'm making this up because I want your *money*?' She stared at him. 'What an appalling accusation, to assume that I would…' Emotion temporarily robbed her of speech. Furious and hurt, she stared at him, utterly appalled. 'I'm having a *baby*. Your baby.'

He actually shuddered. She jerked, almost dropping the phone.

Because the expression in his eyes wasn't about *money*. He had too much of that to be bothered. This was the worst news in the world to him because he didn't want a baby. He didn't want her.

'Okay.' She broke. 'I've told you. That's all I'm obligated to do. You've chosen not to believe me. You don't have to.'

He just stared at her. To her horror, beads of sweat formed on his forehead and the colour leached from his skin. As belief dawned in his eyes, he looked as unwell as she felt. And it wasn't just belief she saw in him. It was *horror*.

Even through the churning nausea of her own despair she saw that change. His jaw was so clamped he was either stuck for something to say or desperately trying to hold back a stream of expletives. She suspected it was the latter.

He shot a look away from the screen. 'I need time to process this.'

'Yep,' she said, desperate to end the call before she vomited.

He was horrified. She was mortified.

'I'll be on the first flight I can.' His words were clipped. 'I'll message you the details.'

He ended the call. He couldn't go fast enough for her nor for himself. She leaned against the wall, her strength evaporating.

It had been a shock for her but it hadn't been the worst thing in the world. That was the thing—she was already past the horror and through to the disbelieving wonder. There was *such* wonder. This was unexpected. But this baby wasn't *unwanted* by her.

The same wasn't true for Massimo. He couldn't have looked more horrified. He'd been so outraged, he'd not believed her—he'd been furious at the thought. Then he'd realised she was telling the truth and he'd not just shut down, he'd been repulsed.

Devastated, Carrie kept replaying the moment he'd believed her. He'd all but shuddered with revulsion. Any last warmth had been snuffed by the nightmare she'd presented him with. He didn't want the baby. He certainly didn't want her. Which meant she was going to be on her own.

Her family would make her feel as if she'd failed, but there wasn't anything terribly new in that. She could handle it. But she wouldn't have her child striving to meet their impossible standards—or then being neglected of attention if she or he wasn't their kind of superstar. So somehow she would make it work. Other people did. They solo-parented all the world over. She could too. Because she *wasn't* a failure. She was just kind of normal.

But right now everything hurt. She curled into a ball on her sofa, trying to stop the incessant replay of that moment but failing. He'd accused her of lying. He'd looked at her with disbelief and disgust. That he'd believed that of her... Had everything she'd felt that night been false? The betrayal *hurt*. She closed her eyes, desperate to wipe the sight of his reaction from her mind, exhausted by the effort of it all.

She woke some time in the pre-dawn hours. It wasn't a crippling, searing pain but a dull ache down low. One she felt every damn month. Fresh tears stung as her sad little heart tore. She still felt sick but figured that was from shame. God, it was so typical that she'd made such a colossal, embarrassing mistake.

Except she hadn't. The test yesterday had been positive. Maybe she'd done it wrong. But she knew she hadn't. She knew, in her bones, that she'd been pregnant. Now she wasn't. And the hurt she'd felt only hours before had nothing on this.

At least *he* didn't have to worry any more.

She couldn't bear to tell him to his face tomorrow. He wouldn't be able to hide his relief, while she wouldn't be able to hide her devastation. Hopefully he'd not yet left for the airport.

She didn't make a video call this time. She sent a simple single text.

Just got my period. Sorry to have concerned you.

She switched off her phone the second she'd sent it. Now they never, *ever* had to see each other again.

CHAPTER FOUR

Seven months later

'BULA VINAKA!' CARRIE smiled at the street vendor and savoured the scent of fresh sliced pineapple, hoping the juicy mix of sweet and acidic would be the invigorating kick she desperately needed. Breakfast hadn't happened. She'd slept badly, only to wake late, and had literally run to work. Fortunately, her boss, Sereana, had suggested they grab a snack before their first meeting.

Around her the market crowd moved amorphously. She pushed back on the lingering discomfort that had robbed her of rest and breathed in the vibrancy. Her contract extension was almost over and she was determined to enjoy every final moment she had in Fiji. She turned, taking in the verdant, vital atmosphere, and a tall figure crossed her vision in the distance. Clad in black, the guy moved with the confidence of someone who owned it all.

Recognition sparked, making her do a double take. Memories flooded, muddying her mind. She'd worked hard to suppress all thoughts of Massimo these last few months, but suddenly she *saw* him.

Surely not? Fiji would be the *last* place he'd appear—he wasn't a beach holiday kind of guy, remember? But Carrie's tired mind tricked her regardless, super-imposing other attributes onto that distant hewn physique—arrogance, sensuality, *challenge*.

She gritted her teeth. She was in the most beautiful place in the world and life was wonderful. She'd moved on from that one night all those months ago, and the mortifying mistake she'd made those few weeks later. But her sun-dazzled eyes kept tracking the figure. Laughter, excitement and energy hummed from the group surrounding him. She blinked away the black spots of sun blindness. Even though he had his back to her, she saw the way his hair fell slightly long and remembered the feel of it between her fingers.

She needed him to turn. Would she see those disturbingly green eyes? Would she see a sensual mouth? If he stepped closer, would she hear a voice that whispered wicked invitation and wilful temptation? All those months ago she'd been so seduced by him, she'd abandoned all caution, all reticence, for a single night of silken ecstasy only to…

A sharp pain lanced, shocking her back to the present. Winded, she pressed her hand to her stomach. How the mind could wreak havoc on the body. The stabbing sensation was a visceral reminder of the desolate emptiness she'd been trying to ignore for so long.

She'd recovered from that heartbreak. She was living her best life here—free and adventurous, bathing in the warm, brilliant waters of the Pacific. Her confusion was because she was tired. But she couldn't resist stepping closer—even as another sharp pain stole her breath.

'That's interesting.' He addressed the man beside him. 'Why are…?'

Shock deadened her senses, muting both him and the pain still squeezing her to the point where she couldn't breathe. That *voice*. The low tone that invited such confidence and tempted the listener to share their deepest secrets.

Massimo hadn't just spoken to her. He'd offered the sort of attention that had simply stupefied her mind and left her able only to say *yes*. And she had. Like all the women who'd come before her. And doubtless all those who'd come after.

Now his brief laugh was deep and infectious. Despite the distance, it was as if he had his head intimately close to hers, his arm around her waist, his lips brushing her highly sensitised skin…

Pain tore through her muscles, forcing her to the present again. She gasped as it seared from her insides and radiated out with increasingly harsh intensity. She stared, helpless in the power of it, as that dark head turned in her direction. His green-eyed gaze arrowed on her.

Massimo.

'Carrie?' Sereana materialised, blocking him from Carrie's view. 'Are you okay?' Her boss looked as alarmed as she sounded.

Carrie crumpled as the cramp intensified. It was as if she'd been grabbed by a ginormous shark that was trying to tear her in two. 'Maybe I ate something…'

Her vision tunnelled as she tumbled to the ground.

'Carrie?'

Not Sereana.

She opened her eyes and stared straight into his. 'Massimo?'

It couldn't really be him. She was hallucinating, surely? But she felt strong arms close about her. She felt herself being lifted and pressed to his broad, hard chest. He was hot and she could hear the thud of his racing heart. Or maybe it was only her own.

If this were just a dream, fine. She closed her eyes and kept them closed. She would sleep and this awful agony would stop. She really needed it to stop.

'Carrie!'

CHAPTER FIVE

'CAN I GET an update on Carrie Barrett's condition please?'

Massimo paced across the office floor while he waited for the hospital receptionist to answer.

'She's listed as serious. I'm sorry, sir, I can't say anything more.'

He closed his eyes. For the first time in almost a week, she'd not been classed as *critical*. Relief warred with frustration. He still didn't know what the hell was wrong with her. Patient privacy rules meant he wasn't cleared to receive information and her doctors had ruled she couldn't have visitors or take calls. He wasn't family. They had no relationship. He was just the guy who'd caught her when she'd collapsed.

It had been terrifying.

She'd not regained consciousness in those horrific minutes when he'd held her as his driver had taken them to the nearest hospital. Medics had met him in the car park. He'd not got inside, and in the confusion he hadn't been able to find out who was the woman she'd been with. Now he was unable to find out anything more than the one-word answer. And he couldn't just leave. He needed to know she was okay. He'd been needing to know that for months. Because of the guilt still roiling in his belly.

The receptionist now recognised his voice and the next day she answered before he'd finished asking.

'She's stable, sir.'

Massimo breathed out. Stable was better than serious. Whatever it was, Carrie was obviously on the mend. Equally obviously, she didn't want him to know more. Because she'd seen him. She'd said his name. But she hadn't contacted him or authorised the hospital to allow him to receive information about her. And maybe, after what had happened, that was understandable. He couldn't bear to remember the last time they'd spoke. Not that shocking video call nor the harrowing message he'd received less than twelve hours later.

Yeah, that guilt still burned. He hadn't just reacted badly to her news on the call, he'd been appalling. And he'd not explained. How could he have said anything to her then? Why add to her obvious distress with his own nightmares of maternal mortality? He knew the facts. What had happened to his mother was rare. But that hadn't stopped his immediate, uncontrollable horror. He hadn't wanted Carrie in any danger.

But the situation had resolved itself. Rapidly. Awfully. Her message had been the end. He should have been able to let it go. Let all thoughts of *her* go. That was obviously what she'd wanted, given she'd cut off her phone. Instead his thoughts had festered. Was it his fault? Had he upset her so much? Was she okay?

So he couldn't just leave her now. He still didn't want her in any danger. How much her condition mattered! It was that lingering guilt, right?

Not entirely, no. He couldn't forget *her*. Hell, she was why he was in Fiji at all. Her joyful dreams of heading to a Pacific island paradise had got to him. He'd not taken her teasing suggestion that he invest there seriously at the time. But a couple of months later he'd still been unable to shake the thought and he'd begun a genuine investigation for work. Now he was feeling raw enough to admit the ridiculous truth. He'd been tempting fate—wanting to find her, unable to forget her. Hell, he still dreamed about her every damn night, and had since the start. It was horrendous.

And she didn't want to see him.

So Massimo had respected her wishes. He'd forced himself to fly home. He couldn't waste more time on something so ludicrously personal. He never had before and he was not going to succumb to obsession in the way of his father. But from Sydney he still made the daily call, indulging that stupid need for the few minutes it took. The need to know how she was. Where she was.

Each day he got the same response. *Stable. Stable. Stable.* Always followed by the kicker, 'I'm sorry, sir, no visitors or calls allowed.'

It was almost another three weeks before everything changed. Because it wasn't the usual receptionist.

'Barrett?' the telephonist echoed vaguely as he tapped on the computer. 'Barrett. They're both doing well.'

Well was good, but... Massimo froze. 'Both?'

'Uh...' The stand-in receptionist sounded hesitant.

But Massimo wasn't losing this nugget of information now. 'Both Barretts?' he confirmed confidently, as if this was exactly what he'd expected. 'Not just Carrie?'

'Yes, both are stable. I'm afraid I can't give any more information, sir.'

'Of course. I understand.'

But he didn't. At all.

He replayed that moment in the market, when he'd been on a tour with some interested advisors. Everything had happened so quickly. She was already on the ground when he'd got to her. He'd not had time to pay close attention to anything other than getting her help. She'd been in a loose summer dress. Maybe she'd been a little softer than she'd been all those months ago, but she hadn't looked obviously *pregnant.*

Now he pulled up the very last message he'd received from Carrie Barrett before her phone had been disconnected. The message that had haunted him every day of the seven months since it had landed.

Just got my period. So sorry to have concerned you.

He'd been awash with regret and guilt the first time he'd read it. But this time? Fury filled him. Because it had been a lie. An absolute, unforgivable lie.

Two weeks later Massimo leaned against the car, his gaze fixed on the automatic doors. He'd been here all day. Yesterday. The day before. He'd be here tomorrow too, if necessary. On the ground he'd chased the rumour and found it was true.

Both stable.

Rage had gripped him so tightly, he'd almost stormed straight into that hospital and swept the child into his arms, ready to eviscerate Carrie with his fury. At the same time sweep *her* into his arms. He wanted to run his hands all over her to ensure she was fine. He needed certainty that both she and the baby were okay. He needed that more than his next damn breath. And that need made him even angrier. He did not want to be so consumed by thoughts of *her*. But how much she must have suffered. To have been in hospital, so long. *Critical…*

But allowing emotion to overwhelm him wasn't going to get him what he wanted. He needed control—not to be locked out, not to be lied to.

It was the *worst*. This meant *family*, meant commitment, meant everything beyond his capability. But he had to ensure their security. So he would. Because Massimo refused to fail. He'd got *himself* under control. And he'd planned. Meticulously.

Carrie rolled her shoulders to loosen the sundress from her skin. The last few weeks had been a blur of confusion, of kindness from people she barely knew and of overwhelming emotion. She just needed five minutes alone before leaving the hospital for good. While she felt physically stronger, mentally she'd only recently emerged from a fog of disbelief. But she had to face what—and who—she'd been avoiding.

Massimo.

She actually thought she'd seen him that day in the market. She'd been in such pain, she'd hallucinated, her mind playing tricks as her body had been compelled to give up its secret. It had been an embarrassingly wishful 'rescue me' fantasy. She'd 'casually' asked Sereana what had happened at the market because she couldn't remember clearly. Sereana had explained that a couple of men had swept her up and brought her to the hospital in a private car, but that she had got left behind and had made her own way there. She'd not known who they were and had not seen them again.

Of course it hadn't been Massimo. Carrie shivered at the prospect of telling him her news now, knowing exactly how much he'd not wanted this.

She walked out of the hospital towards the flame tree marking the edge of the grounds. Its branches were smothered in scarlet flowers, signalling the height of a strong summer. Returning to England and her parents' judgement wasn't an option. As soon as she got to Sereana's house, she'd book her ticket to Australia. She had to do what was right. She'd taken too long already.

'Carrie?'

Great. Now she was hearing him—a conjuring up in her stressed, sleep-deprived state because she'd been thinking of him. Because she was finally well enough to know she couldn't put seeing him off any longer and actually had to do something about it. Because until now she'd had to focus on…

'Carrie.'

She turned, startled.

Massimo Donati-Wells was standing only a few feet away.

Her brain cut out. He *wasn't* a hallucination. He was here. With a raw edge to his voice and ferociousness in his stance. Time ended, just as it had the first night she'd met him. Only now his moss-coloured eyes were icy, his cheekbones like blades, his lethal energy coiled.

She couldn't breathe, unwilling to accept or even define the surfeit of feelings rampaging through her. Equally unable to deny them. Shock-

ingly, one in particular ballooned—an efferves-
cent bubble that couldn't be contained. *Pleasure.*

For a sliver of a second she saw heat flare in
his green gaze, a mirror of the yearning burn
sparking within her. A fleeting wisp of dangerous, dangerous *hope* soared. But the bubble burst
and released true terror. Because Massimo was
not smiling.

Tell him.

Her lips parted but nothing emerged. There
was no breath in her boneless body, no thought
in her cotton-wool brain. She could only stare as
memories surfaced from that locked box deep
inside. They spilled out of order like fragments
of shattered glass—some too perfect, others too
devastating, all too painful to piece together.

Despite her determination to bury all thoughts
of him, every night her subconscious battled her
mental rigor. Every night it won. He appeared in
the dreams she dreaded—the dreams that made
her restless and hot—despite the overhead fan
and her single layer of cotton covering, despite
her heartbreak, despite her massive new responsibilities.

Tell him.

But she remembered the last time she'd done
that. She'd tried for months to wipe it from her

memory. She didn't want to see that expression again now.

You have no choice.

This was the last thing he wanted. *She* was the last thing he wanted. And as for…

Now.

Guilt burned the back of her throat. How could she easily segue into, *Wow, how convenient you're here. I've been meaning to get in touch… there's something I need to tell you…*

How, when he towered, commanding attention, leaner than she remembered? How, when he looked impossibly cool in that shirt, apparently unaffected by humidity or heat or heightened emotion?

There *was* no emotion. Why would there be? They'd had a one-night stand. That was all. He was a master of them. The brilliant billionaire—sleek and successful, oblivious to heat or other pressure, utterly in control. But that sharpness hadn't been there the night they'd met. Nor had there been such an uncompromising set to his jaw.

She should have got in contact with him by now. She should have phoned. But she'd wanted to deal with him in person because she'd been afraid he wasn't going to believe, or understand.

It had taken *her* weeks to understand. Dread poured into her veins, dripping into a bottomless pool of despair.

'You lied to me.' The charming warmth was gone.

He wasn't the man she'd allowed to seduce her in a night so searing she'd not wanted it to end. But the ramifications were unending.

Her voice still wouldn't work. She was unable to utter even an inanity, let alone the truth. He shoved his hands into his pockets. His stance grew increasingly rigid. She could see his fists despite that perfectly cut fabric. No blood beat around her icy body as the horrific realisation hit.

'Are you not going to answer?' His over-enunciated demand excoriated her like a shower of small, sharp stones. 'Can't you tell me the truth even when I'm standing right in front of you?'

'Mass…' She couldn't even say his whole name. Her throat was thick, her brain sluggish. Her words were rusty and weren't the ones she needed to say.

He jerked his head in a negating gesture. 'Liar.' His whisper didn't just cut, it poisoned. An almost inaudible accusation that dripped with scorn. 'You're a *liar.*'

She deserved his anger. She did. But she'd *not*

lied. She needed to explain but she didn't even know where to begin. The truth was so preposterous it had taken her weeks to believe—even when she'd had the proof right in front of her.

'How *could* you?' The fury in him frothed over. 'Stop stalling, Carrie.' He stepped closer and sliced open her worst nightmare. 'You know I'm here for my child. Why are you alone? What have you done with her?'

Massimo had thought he'd moved past anger. He'd thought he'd worked through the white-hot, visceral fury that had scoured him relentlessly over the last two weeks. He'd been so arrogant, he'd thought he was now comfortably cruising in the lane of ice-cold control and that he had been for days as he'd made the final, crucial preparations of his perfect plan.

Wrong. So damned wrong.

One glance into her clear blue eyes, one look at her soft lips and elfin chin, one whiff of her floral sensuality, one tiny moment in the same space as her and he was tossed back into the maelstrom of rage that had been shredding him for days.

How could someone so deceitful be so angelically beautiful? With one look, with barely one word, she had destroyed his equanimity. He, who

managed difficult people and tense contract ne-
gotiations, apparently couldn't stand two seconds in her company without falling victim to
his emotions. The instant surge of rage was almost impossible to control.

Rage *was* the emotion. There was *nothing* else.
Certainly not some damned flare of… *No*. She'd
betrayed him completely and he did not *want* her.
He wanted only to do what was necessary, what
was *right*.

The teal dress hid her curves but highlighted
the clarity of her eyes. They'd widened while the
rest of her petite features had become pinched.
Pallor dulled her radiance as fear stripped away
her customary soft, smiling welcome.

'Where is she?' he asked tensely.

'In the hospital.'

'And you've abandoned her?'

'No!'

'Then why are you out here alone? Take me
to her.' Her shocked expression infuriated him
and that supposed control slipped. 'I know she's
mine.'

Her eyes widened. 'How…?'

'Do you expect me to believe that, within a day
of gifting your virginity to me, you were off having unprotected sex with an assortment of other

men?' he snapped. 'Maybe you did. Maybe that was all part of your plan.'

Her jaw dropped. 'What plan? There was no plan.'

Pure deceit dripped from her tongue. He drew a sharp breath as his anger railed against the tight bonds he fought to secure it with. There'd been too many liars in his life already, liars who'd razed his world to the ground. That wasn't happening again.

'You expect me to believe that?' He tightened his fists in his pockets, pushed close to losing control. He had to shove every other muscle into a kind of stasis.

How could he be surprised that Carrie Barrett could lie right to his face without even blinking or blushing? She'd been lying for months. He had to restrain himself from pacing closer, from shouting out the frustration that had amassed since he'd found out the appalling truth. He'd play this as coolly as he'd planned.

But just looking at her derailed his thoughts. The bright sundress didn't suit her sleepless, worry-ravaged visage. She didn't look as if she'd been living it up on the beach. Any tan she'd managed to acquire had faded during these weeks in hospital. Tiredness muted her. She looked vulnerable and that made him feel guilty. No. *She* was the guilty one.

'Did you lie about everything?' His control slipped again. 'About your virginity? Maybe you're *that* good an actress.'

Fierce rejection flooded his body even as he spoke. He didn't know why he was torturing himself but seeing her in the flesh brought forth all the memories he'd been failing to suppress. Right now his bloody brain replayed the moment when he'd claimed first possession—when he'd stared so closely into her blue eyes and watched so carefully for her response. He'd never drawn such deep pleasure in bringing a lover to that peak, again and again. She'd been so eager, so gorgeous, she'd turned him inside out in seconds.

They'd only had one night. He rarely had more with a woman—a deliberate choice to avoid emotional entanglement. But he'd not slept with another woman since Carrie. It had been the best part of a *year*. Never had he gone without for so long. Appallingly, even now in the face of her lies, with the full extent of her betrayal revealed, his body still wanted hers. As if hauling her against him could possibly salve the wounds she'd inflicted!

Fool.

He'd waited these last two weeks—pacing while preparing, hoping against hope that she would initiate contact, that she would seek him out and show some skerrick of integrity. She hadn't. Her true character had been revealed. She'd chosen this path and, now he knew what he was up against, *he* had to do all that was necessary. Which meant sticking to *his* plan. The ends absolutely justified the means.

A bruised mix of accusation and hurt shadowed her eyes. She drew a steadying breath and he knew she was about to brave it. The gesture stirred another unwanted memory. The night they'd met she'd been let down but she'd lifted her head and ordered that cocktail, determined not to show her humiliation even though it had been obvious. Just as her emotion was obvious now. Why had she wanted to hide from him? What was her agenda?

Massimo wanted the truth, no matter the price—moral or otherwise. 'Don't bother trying to lie more. You know I can see through your bravado,' he said bitterly. It was far too late for that.

'I was going to tell you.' She finally spoke. A whispery confession that still wasn't the truth.

He had to hold his muscles so rigid he couldn't

even roll his eyes. He didn't want to hear more of her lies, but as for honesty? He realised too late that there was nothing she could say that would make this okay.

She stepped towards him, her words tumbling faster. 'You have to understand—'

'How?' Fury got the better of him and he viciously hurled the word at her. 'How am I *ever* supposed to do that? You told me you were pregnant. Then you told me you weren't. No, wait—you didn't even bother to tell me, you just sent a message and disappeared. You went completely offline, unable to be contacted. Turns out you moved to some remote Pacific island to enjoy your pregnancy alone and have your baby in secret. Weeks later you *still* haven't told me. How can I ever understand any of that? What the hell is going on, Carrie?'

She laced her fingers together and slowly shook her head in continued denial, her heartbreakingly blue eyes beseeching. 'I didn't…'

He waited, his muscles burning.

'I didn't know…'

She only managed one more word before her voice petered out again.

'Didn't know what—how to get in touch with

me?' Impatiently he stepped closer. 'I gave you my *personal* number.'

She gaped at him for a second and sudden defiance flashed in her eyes. 'Should I consider myself honoured?'

'Absolutely.' He glared at her. He rarely gave that number to anyone. 'Why didn't you call?' he snapped. 'You know I wanted to do right by you.'

A stricken look flickered in her face.

'You've had *months*!' he erupted, retaliating against the tug in his chest at her expression. 'And there are no excuses. Nothing you can say can adequately explain what you've done.'

He hated that he sounded wounded. He didn't want her to know how badly her actions had bothered him—he didn't even want to admit that to himself. He'd claw back his self-control and focus on the only thing that mattered—the welfare of the baby she'd hidden from him. Children had never been in his plan and still weren't. But, while fate had other ideas, he wasn't having Carrie steal his remaining choices. She could think what she liked of him. That was *her* problem, not his.

'Are you going to take her from me?' she asked brokenly.

Her. His daughter.

Massimo stared at her, struggling with the burning sensation deep in his gut. Rage warred with empathy. Her widened eyes were almost feverishly bright. Terror emanated from her in an oppressive, desperate wave that he couldn't turn his back on. He gritted his teeth and mustered every speck of control, of unwilling compassion, that he could.

'You might think it's acceptable to take a child from a parent without so much as a word. I, however, do not,' he muttered hoarsely.

The breath she released blew like a stormy gust but it cleared none of the tense air between them. His pulse raced, tumultuous and unpredictable—as his feelings concerning her apparently were. They surged like tumble weed. He didn't want *feelings*. They weren't conducive to his plan. Emotions—intense emotions—destroyed everything. They had before.

Stay on track. Stay calm.

He wanted to turn from her fear but couldn't. It was so thick, it encapsulated her—as if she were stuck in a smeared glass dome that he itched to smash so he could free her, see her properly. But *he* was who she was afraid of.

It rankled more than it should have. Of course, she *should* be afraid. She should wonder what he might do now. Who would blame him for this anger considering what she'd done? But *why* had she done it?

There was the rub. There was the unanswered question.

He didn't want to care. She was just the lying, secretive mother of the child he'd not wanted. And there was the *real* problem. The *last* thing he wanted was to be left solely responsible for the baby. She needed his assets, but not him personally. He didn't have the skills to parent. He'd not had the example. And honestly? He didn't have the desire. Relationships were not something he managed. Emotional intimacy? No, not something he was capable of. But that child would know the *truth* of her parentage. Massimo would provide all he *could*.

Stability and security mattered. But right now nothing mattered as much as the truth. 'Why did you lie about losing the baby?'

She was very still now. 'I didn't lie.'

Massimo briefly closed his eyes in frustrated disbelief at her quiet, determined reply because it rang so damned true. And then to his fury she went one further.

'I've never lied to you.'

CHAPTER SIX

CARRIE WINCED AS Massimo opened his eyes and shot her a look of such condemnation that she should have instantly been eviscerated.

'This is a waste of time. We need to leave.' He growled.

Her heart thundered. 'To—?'

'Get out of this heat,' he interrupted, his energy unleashed. 'You look like you're about to pass out.'

But she planted herself in front of him. 'I *didn't* lie.'

She'd just not told him some things. Yes, some very *important* things, but she'd wanted to tell him in person. In those first days she'd been too unwell to think, let alone act. More recently she'd coped only by focussing moment by moment. 'It all happened so fast—'

'Pregnancies aren't all that fast,' he interrupted before she could fully explain. Those lines of condemnation deepened. 'You could have found five minutes to call…'

He was so angry, he was unable to listen let alone believe. The warm, attentive man from all those months ago was the mirage. The *reality* of Massimo was right in front of her. The one she'd seen on that video call. The one who'd believed the very worst of her. Untrusting. Uncaring. Implacable. Impatient. Her fear had been so very justified. He was going to be ruthless and relentless in pursuing what he wanted. And he wasn't going to give her a chance.

And, at the same time as her fear exploded, guilt crashed in on a tsunami that smashed what little confidence she had left. Because she had messed up. If he'd only give her a few seconds to explain. But that was her own fault too, wasn't it? She'd had weeks to do that and she hadn't. *That* was on her.

It was no excuse, but the physical weakness had wrecked her in ways she was still coming to terms with, and Massimo appearing so unexpectedly had shocked her into an unthinking, reactionary response.

'I'm sorry,' she said desolately. 'I should have got in touch. I promise I was going to. *Please* let me explain.'

His jaw clamped and he jerked his chin—assent full of resentment.

It was going to sound preposterous. Why she'd not reached out already—not to him or to any family or friends, beyond the few she'd made here.

'When I messaged you, I truly believed I'd got my period,' she explained flatly. 'I didn't know I was still pregnant until I went into labour at the market here a few weeks ago.'

The morning she'd thought she'd seen him. That unforgettably hot day when she and Sereana had stopped for a snack before a meeting.

Massimo didn't move. She began to wonder if he'd even heard her. She was about to repeat herself when he finally spoke.

'Is *that* what you're going with?' Contempt tarred the bitterest laugh she'd ever heard. 'How do you expect me to believe that?'

'I can't make you believe anything.' She drew deep, summoning dignity to suppress the tears stinging her eyes. 'But it's the truth.'

'How could you not know? Not in all those months of pregnancy?' He put his hands on his hips and glared at her. 'Didn't you gain weight? *Show?*'

'Not initially.' Her skin burned. It was *obvious* she'd gained some weight. 'And then I thought I was just enjoying the food here. I wasn't focused on trying to stay fit or anything.'

She'd avoided scales and mirrors for a long while, as coconut *brûlée* had become a favourite treat. Okay, there'd been some comfort eating. She was human and she'd been hurt and she'd wanted to forget things. And she'd had minor erratic bleeding, but she'd figured her system was taking a while to regulate again after the loss. Honestly, most of the time she'd tried hard not to think about it.

'I know how unbelievable it sounds. *I* still can't believe it and I'm the one who's—' She broke off as she saw him tense. 'No one is more aware of how stupid this makes me seem. But why would I do this? Why *wouldn't* I tell you?'

'That's what I've been wondering.' Hot fury flashed in his eyes. He hated her right now.

'You're Massimo Donati-Wells, Australian billionaire genius. If I'm the awful woman you obviously think me, wouldn't I want you to know? Wouldn't I be out to get everything I could from you?'

'For all I know you might still be,' he countered crisply. 'This might be part of your plan to extract exactly that.'

'I don't want anything from you,' she snapped.

'Would I choose to collapse in a public market? Would I choose to give birth unknowing and utterly unprepared? I didn't know anything—not even how to change a nappy, let alone feed and properly care for a tiny baby. It was terrifying.'

He was somehow nearer, somehow taller, somehow even angrier—grinding out his condemnation. 'If you hadn't run away in the first place, that *never* would have happened.'

She'd been dreading explaining her pathetic mistake to anyone. Who would believe that even *she* had been that stupid and naive? Then again, she'd believed her ex-fiancé when he'd said he wanted to wait until they were married to have sex when all the while he'd been off having sex with…

Don't think about that now.

She'd been so confused when she'd first woken—more than two days after Ana's delivery. Apparently she wasn't the first woman to have claimed she 'didn't know she was pregnant'. When she'd first regained consciousness and expressed her total shock, one of the doctors had sat beside her with patronising kindness, repeatedly telling her she wasn't to feel ashamed at being an unwed mother, and that she didn't need to make up such an outlandish tale. She could just admit the truth...

But she *genuinely* hadn't known she was pregnant. She'd *grieved* all those months ago. And she'd grieved over Massimo. She'd run away from Auckland that very night because she hadn't wanted to face him, had been afraid that, if she did, he'd see how desperately she'd wanted their unplanned child when he so desperately *hadn't*.

Massimo stared into her eyes, a frown in his. 'When you thought you'd miscarried, you didn't see a doctor for confirmation?'

'It was so early on I didn't think I needed to,' she mumbled.

She'd not wanted to be baldly told the truth by some doctor she didn't know. She'd just wanted to escape. She'd come to Fiji early and told herself it was all going to be okay...eventually.

'Why didn't you care for yourself enough to get checked out?' he asked roughly.

Massimo's question threw her. He wasn't judging her for not realising she'd still been pregnant, but...

Why didn't you care for yourself enough...?

Now she felt worse. Not only did no one else really care, *she* hadn't cared for *herself*. And there was no answer she could give him.

'I was already on a flight from Sydney when I got that message, but when I landed, you'd vanished.'

Another layer of guilt piled on. Because, yes, she'd run away. Truthfully, she still didn't want him to know how much he'd impacted on her decision to go. She'd fallen beneath his spell. But now? He couldn't think less of her anyway.

'I didn't want to burden you with my emotions,' she said shakily. 'We barely knew each other.'

'Even so, you didn't think I'd have supported you?'

He made it sound as if *he'd* actually cared. That stoked her anger.

'You didn't want the baby, Massimo,' she said. 'You *know* you didn't. You were so shocked and appalled, you couldn't get off that call quickly enough.'

His expression shuttered. 'I wanted to know *you* were okay but you blew me off. I would have paid for the doctors if I'd known you were struggling. I would have taken you to see one myself.'

Sure, he was courteous, and he'd wanted to ensure her physical well-being. He was decent enough guy. But all she'd been to him was a novelty one-night stand. He'd not wanted anything more. Certainly not a literally life-long connection. Because he didn't deny her first truth. He hadn't wanted their child.

He muttered an oath beneath his breath and she felt his shift in thinking—from anger to wary concern.

'Even if I believe you about the pregnancy—and I'm not saying I do—it's been seven weeks since you gave birth. Why haven't you been in touch since? I phoned that hospital every day. You must know that.'

'What?' She gaped at him. 'No one told me you'd called. How did you know I was in hospital?

'Seriously?' He gaped at her. 'I *took* you there.'

Her vision tunnelled. 'You really were at the market?'

He gaped, raw fury firing his words. 'You called my name.'

'I thought I'd hallucinated you,' she whispered. 'I thought that was a dream. Because after... after...'

It had been days before she'd regained consciousness, then she'd been overwhelmed by caring for Ana. The doctors had been concerned by her agitation, her supposed confusion and refusal to admit she'd been pregnant. They'd not even let Sereana visit her for several days. 'No one mentioned any calls,' she said. 'Surely they would have passed on your messages?'

His jaw clamped. 'I didn't leave a message. I didn't leave my name.'

'Why not?' She was stunned.

'I didn't think I needed to.' He growled. 'You'd seen me at the market.'

'But I didn't think that was real.'

He hesitated. 'I didn't realise you were that confused at the time. But why didn't you call me in the days after?'

'I got rid of my phone in New Zealand. I didn't have your number here. Besides, it wasn't something I could tell you on a call. Not this time.'

'Yet you've not booked a flight.'

'How do you know?' She felt angry and confused. 'Have you been spying on me?'

'You've hardly given me reason to trust you,' he justified. But his body tensed. 'People lie.'

'*I* didn't,' she said, drawing in a hard breath. 'I just didn't tell you.'

'Isn't that the same thing?'

She shook her head. 'I was scared.'

His mouth tightened. 'You trusted me enough to sleep with me when you hadn't with anyone else.'

'That was different.'

That had just been about her, and *she* was used to rejection. It had been a risk she'd taken for herself. But Massimo had already rejected their baby once and she'd not wanted to see that rejection again. Because, while rejection for herself hurt enough, seeing her baby rejected, not valued—not happening. She wasn't having what had happened to her happen to her daughter. And he'd already rejected their baby once.

She saw his ferocity return and stepped in before he could ask. 'Maybe I should have got medical care all those months ago,' she admitted. 'But I didn't want to face it. Or you. I'm not proud of that. Ana's birth was shocking, and my world went *crazy*. She was little and needed support and I...' She couldn't even remember those first few nights.

'You shouldn't have been alone.'

'I wasn't,' she hastened to reassure him. 'We had the best care. My friend Sereana has been a huge support. Everyone here has been generous and caring. They've been wonderful.'

Far from reassured, he looked angrier. 'Well, now I guess it's my turn to be generous and caring and *wonderful*,' he said sarcastically. 'I already told you I'm here for the baby. And, as at this point in her life, *you're* part of the package, so that means you're coming too. Now.'

At this point in her life?

Did that mean that at some point in the future he expected Carrie *wouldn't* be part of the package?

Fear transformed into fight and Carrie—who usually wouldn't argue with anyone, who would simply smile and say, *Sure!* To whatever was requested because she was such a damned people-pleaser—now stood her ground. Even as she shook while doing so.

'No,' she said harshly. 'I'm not leaving with you.'

Not without knowing where, why and for how long. Not without some *say* in it.

'No?'

Carrie stiffened her legs to stop them trembling. 'I have friends here.'

'And you think they'll rescue you from my evil clutches?' He shook his head sceptically. 'Are they aware that you've denied your child's father *everything*—right down to knowledge of her existence?'

Nausea roiled in her stomach. 'They'll assume I have my reasons for not wanting to be with you.'

She'd made a massive mistake but she couldn't

cede *all* control to him. He'd interpreted everything awfully and her own bitter hurt cut deep. Worse, another tension still strained. Another source of crackling energy that was so wrong. Because, even when icily furious, Massimo was gorgeous and her stupid, *stupid* body didn't want to resist him.

'What are they?' he asked softly. 'How terrible will you make them—make *me*—out to be?' His expression tightened. 'What did I do to make you *this* determined to cut me from the child's life?'

She'd never intended to cut him from Ana's life, but his reaction now... He still wouldn't believe her...

'You don't *want* her!' she snapped angrily. 'You didn't believe me all those months ago. And you *still* think I just want your money.'

What had *she* done to make him that mistrustful of her?

'Yeah?' Fury flashed in his eyes as he snapped back. 'Because I do have money, Carrie. I have unlimited resources. My lawyers will make a compelling case for full custody. You'll be labelled as a mother who was so neglectful she didn't even *know* she was pregnant, who then didn't bother to even try to get in touch with the father, who didn't have a home to bring her child to from hospital... How can you think you'll win?'

She wouldn't. Not when he stacked it like that. Her behaviour sounded appalling and unworthy. But there was no mention of the post-birth complications, the illness, the exhaustion and extenuating circumstances.

But she wasn't about to use her health to manipulate him into pitying her. All those months ago she'd had no idea how powerful he really was. Now she knew more—he was a billionaire boy-wonder who'd made his first millions by 'playing' with investments as a teen. He'd formed his own private equity company specialising in structuring deals for start-ups, then for firms needing to expand. Frankly, she didn't understand it entirely. But the several spotlight articles she'd read had stressed his work ethic. Detail on his personal life had been scant in those articles. But photos of him out with a bunch of different women littered Sydney city-life blogs. *That* hadn't surprised her at all.

She understood he was driven, not just to achieve, but to *accumulate*. To win at all costs. She needed to break through to him.

'You said you weren't going to take her from me,' she said.

There was a moment of electric silence. She stared into his furious green eyes, reading the swirl of emotion that he couldn't suppress.

'And I'm not,' he said eventually. 'But compromise takes two and I'll take what I'm *owed*. So come with me now, or I'll call the police and kick up such merry hell you won't know what's hit you. *Nothing* will stand in the way of what I want. Certainly not you.'

Some *compromise*. It was an unadulterated, vicious ultimatum.

So, she had to push. 'And what is it, exactly, that you want?'

He paused again. 'I want what's best for the child. I want to work through this *with* you. There's no need for this to be acrimonious. The least you can give me right now is time. I think I deserve just a little of that, given how much I've already missed out on.' Massimo growled. 'You need time. You look tired.'

His brusque assessment diminished her. She must have mistaken the flicker of heat in his eyes when she'd first seen him. It was mortifying that she was still so wishful for his attention. That she was still so blown away by him that she'd read anger as lust.

Pull it together. The only person who mattered now was Ana.

'I assume you have room in a hotel somewhere?' she asked.

He lifted his head like a gleaming warrior sensing victory. Triumph flashed in his mossy eyes. 'Room for all of us, yes.'

'Which hotel? Ana and I can meet you there.'

'Do you honestly think I'm going to let you out of my sight?' His brief laugh was mirthless. 'I wouldn't put it past you to vanish again.'

How little he trusted her. But she didn't trust him either. He assumed. He judged. And he wanted to control. But Massimo Donati-Wells wasn't going to get everything his own way. Because Carrie had a purpose bigger than herself. She had her daughter to protect.

'Then let's go.' Folding her arms across her chest, she held herself tightly. 'You need to meet Ana.'

CHAPTER SEVEN

MASSIMO STRODE TOWARDS the hospital entrance, hyper-conscious of Carrie silent alongside him. She was so close and yet so damned distant.

I was scared.

Why? Had she sensed the danger within him? Did she somehow know he wasn't capable of sticking as a father? Was that why she'd just spun him such a tale? Yet, impossible as her story was, part of him believed her. It incensed him that she'd faced any of this alone. That she'd not sought help all those months ago, suffering needless stress. Putting herself and the child at *risk*. It was unforgivable.

Plus the fact that his damned body couldn't care less whether she'd lied to him or not. All it wanted was for him to lie *with* her. For the first time, the afternoon heat bothered him. He wanted to peel off the shirt sticking to his back. Even though she'd agreed to come with him his tension now worsened. He'd not envisaged *this* moment—seeing the baby. Figuring out how he was going to be a father.

Carrie hadn't been wrong. He didn't want children. He never had. His family weren't meant to, after all. They weren't good at caring for them. Massimo was a prime example of both those truths. He was the child that his mother had struggled to conceive and hadn't been able to stay for; the child his father had initially neglected and ultimately abandoned. How the hell was he going to be a decent parent when he'd come from that?

He followed Carrie down the corridor. She greeted the staff by name and they responded with wide smiles. Her awareness and appreciation of them seemed genuine, and they certainly responded to her.

'Dr Taito,' she murmured as they arrived on the maternity ward.

'Carrie.'

Doctor.

Massimo stopped walking. So did the white-coat-clad woman.

Carrie realised and then turned reluctantly. 'Doctor, this is Massimo. Ana's father.'

The doctor stiffened and turned to cast a measuring eye over him. 'I'm sure you're looking forward to meeting your daughter, Massimo.'

His jaw ached from being held so tightly. 'Yes.'

The doctor glanced at Carrie. 'Sereana is waiting with her.'

Carrie smiled awkwardly and moved past. But, as Massimo went to follow, the doctor stopped him with a clinical hand on his arm and a cold stare.

'Carrie had a very tough time,' she said. 'She needs rest.'

Massimo stared back. 'Do you have a moment to talk more?'

The doctor nodded brusquely. 'Absolutely.'

Carrie awkwardly watched Massimo talking quietly with the doctor and wished she had bat ears. She'd not realised they were going to stop outside the room and continue a hushed conversation *without* her, but she couldn't go back and butt in.

Sereana and one of the nurses were now on either side of her, full of excitement about Ana's imminent discharge from the hospital and the surprise arrival of Massimo. Avid curiosity sparkled in their eyes and their smiles were broad. She could hardly create a *scene*. They'd already guessed he was Ana's father. One look at him now, and they were as delighted as if this were a fairy-tale ending to the drama. But it wasn't like that at all.

Moments later Massimo walked in without the doctor. To Carrie's horror, he flashed a full wattage smile at Sereana and spoke before Carrie had a chance to say anything.

'You must be Sereana. I understand I have much to thank you for. I'm very sorry I wasn't able to be here sooner.'

Had the doctor just given him a personality transplant? Now he was all polite charm, the fury completely masked. Predictably, Sereana's eyes widened and, while her mouth opened, no words emerged. Massimo had that effect.

Carrie's heart sank. He'd won already. She only half-listened as Massimo thanked Sereana again and explained that he was now here to take care of everything. Sereana was so stunned by him, she didn't realise he'd smoothly manoeuvred her into leaving sooner than she'd intended. Honestly, Carrie knew it was for the best. She and Massimo needed to work through this on their own.

'I can't thank you enough. You've been so kind to me.' Carrie hugged her friend goodbye. 'I'm so sorry—'

'You've nothing to apologise for!' Sereana interrupted. 'And you kept working on the schedule even when you were laid up in bed!'

Working on their upcoming athletics event had been the one thing Carrie *could* do to say thank you. 'I'll take the laptop with me so I can keep going.'

'I think you have other things to focus on.' Sereana's gaze arrowed to Massimo again.

'I *want* to finish it,' Carrie said quickly.

But Sereana was focused on everything else. 'I'm so glad he's come for you,' she murmured as she hugged her again. 'You should have sent for him *so* much sooner!'

Carrie agreed, but not for the reasons her friend was obviously assuming. But the delighted relief in Sereana's eyes was obvious. Carrie hadn't realised she'd been such a cause of concern for her friend, but of course she had. More than that, maybe she'd been a burden. So she smiled and hid her private concerns. She'd sort everything out just with Massimo.

Once they were alone, Massimo crossed the room, but she caught his quick glance into Ana's cot before he stood by her luggage.

'Is this everything?' His voice sounded husky.

Carrie didn't immediately reply. Tiny and utterly perfect, Ana had completely stolen her heart the second she'd clapped eyes on her. But Massimo hadn't glanced at the baby for more than a millisecond. Carrie's fear mushroomed into something unwieldy and out of control. She knew too well what it was like to be overlooked by the people who should love you unconditionally. She wanted *family* always to come first—ahead of work or other ambition. She wanted Ana to be as valued as she should be. Because Carrie hadn't been and she knew how much it hurt.

'Do you want to hold her?' she asked quietly. And, yes, it was a test.

Massimo stiffened. 'My finally meeting her, weeks late, is not a moment for public viewing.' He nodded towards the open curtain through which she could see the staff standing at their work station, from where they were not so surreptitiously staring.

Chastened, hot emotion engulfed Carrie.

'You bring her. I'll carry the bags. Is that all the luggage there is?' Again, he shot her bag a disparaging glance.

'I travel light and I was going to buy more for Ana once I—'

'It's fine. I've already bought what's required.' He cut her off.

His expression was so shuttered, she didn't ask

what he meant by 'required'. Instead, she carefully lifted Ana.

The hospital farewells were a blur. Once outside, Carrie fumbled to figure how to click the safety harness in the baby seat already installed in Massimo's waiting car. Apparently, she needed a specialist engineering degree. With a stifled growl, Massimo brushed her fumbling fingers aside and swiftly made the contraption click. But then for a timeless moment he paused, his gaze fixed on the baby. Because, in the gentle movement, Ana stirred and her sweet eyes opened.

Carrie had believed that lots of babies had bluish eyes when first born. That their true colour settled a few months in. But Ana's eye colour was strikingly vibrant and—Carrie hoped—fixed. Because her beautiful little eyes were the exact mossy shade of her father's.

Undeniably his eyes. Undeniably *his* child.

Massimo turned and his gaze clashed with Carrie's. His green eyes now almost glowed with an edge that silenced her. Hot and terrifyingly intense. She saw protectiveness. *Possessiveness.*

Carrie's throat constricted. Her heart constricted. Her whole body went on hold—afraid and yet hoping so *hard* for some kind of acceptance. But he said nothing, and Carrie was too choked to.

They drove for only ten minutes then stopped at an island transport service. A helicopter was parked on the pad, its engine already roaring. Butterflies were instantly on a rotor beneath Carrie's ribs. A helicopter felt precarious. Everything was happening too fast and was too far from her control.

Massimo helped unfasten the baby seat and Carrie lifted it. He touched the small of her back with a lightly guiding hand, sensing her reluctance.

'I wouldn't be getting in if I didn't think it was safe,' he said softly. 'I like living. I have a lot to live for.'

Up close she saw it wasn't one of the usual island-hopping helicopters. This one was larger. Its midnight exterior gleamed while the interior was sleek. Once in, Carrie perched on the luxurious leather seat while Massimo secured Ana's baby seat and then took the seat opposite. There were no heads sets so she guessed the cabin must be soundproofed.

'Carrie.' He regarded her intensely as she felt them ascend. 'Breathe.'

She should be looking at her daughter, or at

least the view as they left Suva, but she couldn't break free from Massimo's gaze. There was such intensity and judgement. But, as his gaze held hers, it morphed into wordless reassurance. She wasn't alone in this. Not any more. He was going nowhere. And, while that was concerning in some ways, it also gave her something to depend on.

And then there was something else again.

Her body contracted in reaction. She always yearned for that spark. Fear transformed into slow-building exhilaration. Into energy. She got a full charge from just one long look.

He was *here* and suddenly she was flooded with…

Ana snuffled. The small noise short-circuited the electricity arcing between them. Carrie immediately turned to check on her, hugely relieved to sever the connection, half-disappointed at the same time. Her heart melted at the sight of her daughter's sweet face with her perfect, petite lashes resting on her cheek. She had Massimo's hair colouring too—tiny jet lashes, and downy wisps of dark hair on her head. Carrie stroked her soft cheek in the lightest graze of reassurance. 'Hey, sweetheart.'

With a little turn of her tiny head, Ana blinked

slowly a couple of times before her eyes closed and she slept again. A wave of protectiveness surged through Carrie, another of such gratitude that she'd made it.

When Carrie looked back, Massimo was intently focused on the view out of the window. There was no look between them now—no shared acknowledgment of the heart-melting adorableness of their baby with her full, pink cheeks. That rush of exhilaration was obliterated. It hurt to breathe deeply. Rejection? Being ignored? She'd do anything to spare her child those wounds. His reticence to engage with Ana was only because he wanted privacy, right?

Carrie could scarcely concentrate as they soared over the water. Islands dotted the brilliant blue waters beneath them like emerald and gold jewels—breathtakingly, unbelievably beautiful. Eventually they neared one small island, the sort upon which was only one exclusive resort. Privacy would *definitely* be ensured here.

The sandy beach encircling the island was a stunning creamy gold while the forest area rising in the centre was verdant and lush. Tucked in the plantings on the left stood a group of jaw-dropping buildings, the central villa a vision.

'This is Karakarawa Island,' Massimo said when they landed.

He hopped out of the helicopter and then turned, holding out his hand to offer her support.

His grip was firm and the immediate sizzle sent her straight back to that night. To heat, laughter and the most sensual experience ever. In the mêlée of memories, she barely noticed a man lift her bags and head along the path. But she did see a middle-aged woman in a crisp, white uniform approaching them with a deferential smile.

Wary, Carrie tensed and tugged her hand from Massimo's.

'Leah will take the baby in while I show you around,' Massimo said firmly.

Carrie watched the woman unclasp Ana's baby seat with expert ease.

'Leah is a fully qualified paediatric nurse,' Massimo added.

The woman smiled at Carrie. 'We'll be waiting in the nursery for you.'

Her Australian accent was obvious. Carrie's heart raced. Had Massimo brought Leah to Fiji with him? A nanny to whom he could entrust Ana's care—did that mean he could return to Australia with Ana but *without* Carrie?

'I won't be a moment.' Carrie anxiously

watched Leah carry Ana away. She couldn't ignore the presence of the vital, ruthless man beside her.

'Leah's room is room right next to the nursery,' Massimo said. 'She also has a monitor, so she'll be there when the baby wakes in the night.'

'I'll tend to Ana at night. She needs me.'

His jaw tightened. 'But *you* need undisturbed sleep.'

Their eyes met. She refused to bend on this. But, as she stared at him, other things suddenly entered her mind. *Undisturbed sleep?* Heat scalded as inappropriate thoughts sneaked into her mind like inappropriate bandits. She actually envisioned being with him again.

Idiot! She dropped her gaze. Lingering lust was the last thing she needed. There was too much to sort out to add such distraction to the mix. Berating herself, she barely listened to Massimo as he led her along the neatly trimmed path towards the stunning building, pointing out amenities as they went. But after a moment she realised there was no one else in sight—no one using the beach shades or swimming in the pool, no one having an afternoon drink at the bar… It was extremely, *oddly* quiet.

'Where are the other guests?' she asked as they entered the large main building.

'There aren't any.'

'Did you hire the whole resort?'

A sharp glint shone in his eyes before he blinked back to bland.

'Massimo?' She stopped dead. 'Do you *own* this resort?''

A muscle in his jaw flexed, making his cheek bones impossibly sharper. 'I do now.'

So, it was a recent purchase. Back in Auckland, when they'd met, they'd sparred over the merits of island holidays. She'd been Team Beach while he'd declared them boring. He was all business.

'Are you telling me you bought this island 'specially for...?' She couldn't quite finish the thought. It was preposterous.

'It guarantees privacy and ensures we have everything we need while we're here.'

Who on earth just went and bought an *island*—one with a luxury accommodation complex, swimming pool and all sorts of indulgent amenities?

'How long do you anticipate we'll stay?' She was standing still but she couldn't seem to catch her breath.

'As long as it takes for us to be in agreement regarding the child's future.'

In agreement? Her skin felt too small. They came from different sides of the world and were light years apart in wealth and status. *How* could she hold her own against him? Any agreement would simply be what *he* wanted.

'There's a skeleton staff on the island.' He continued his tour of his newly purchased paradise. 'Apart from Leah, their accommodation is on the other side of the pool. There's plenty of water, plenty of food. There's a satellite phone, also Wi-Fi.'

The last thing Carrie wanted was to go online. It was easier to avoid her family if she didn't. She *definitely* planned to tell them about Ana face to face. Presented with the delicate perfection of her baby, they couldn't *possibly* think she was any kind of mistake. But she couldn't resist provoking Massimo now.

'So I can email an SOS?' she drawled.

'Because you're so good at asking for help when you most need it?' He shot her a look. 'Go right ahead. I'm not afraid of people knowing where you are, who you're with and why. *I* have nothing to hide.'

He led her up to a vast, shaded wooden deck

with a stunning view over the beach. They walked up the stairs towards the open doors and into a large, airy room. 'This is the nursery.'

She paused on the threshold. There was space in here for a *dozen* babies. There was a beautiful cot with hand-stitched cotton coverings and a hand-crafted mobile hanging near a carved rocking chair. Alongside the incredible pieces of artisan carpentry, there was a medical-grade neonatal bassinet and accompanying supplies. That shocked her. The room was totally over-equipped. He'd provided things she wouldn't even have *thought* of, let alone had the money to purchase. It had all just been done, here and organised, *including* round-the-clock care for Ana. Did he need *her* to be here at all?

Leah placed a freshly changed Ana into the cot. 'I'll return later.' She politely smiled and left the room.

Carrie walked straight to Ana. She was happily gazing up at the gorgeous mobile. Carrie's heart puckered as she waited for Massimo to join her beside their baby.

'You've provided so much,' Carrie eventually mumbled. 'Ana doesn't need…'

'I didn't have the luxury of knowing what

might be necessary, so I bought everything with me from Australia,' he said coolly.

Including that hyper-efficient nanny. Carrie swallowed and glanced across at him. 'How long have you been here?'

'A week.'

'You didn't see me sooner?'

'I wasn't on your visitor list, remember? I've been waiting at the hospital for Ana to be discharged,' he said grimly.

'You were waiting outside the whole week?'

'I watched the door while working from the car. Don't worry. I can do a lot via phone. And I had things to arrange. Especially when it became evident that you weren't about to get in touch.'

He'd been ruthlessly cool-headed as he'd worked out his plan.

But she'd intended to get in touch. As soon as she got Ana to Sereana's, she'd been going to book the flight. One look at Massimo's hardened face told her there was no point trying to convince him of that. Too little, too late.

'Your room is in the wing on the other side of this. You can't miss it.' He stepped backwards. 'There are some essentials supplied for you too. I'll leave you to get settled.'

'Don't you want to hold Ana now we're alone?' Her throat tightened.

A muscle flicked in his jaw. 'Later. I have an urgent matter to attend to.'

Her blood iced and she felt it as pure rejection. Why was he determined to be in Ana's life if he wasn't interested in getting to *know* her? The memory of his reaction to news of her pregnancy flashed in her mind. He didn't want children. He didn't want Ana.

'We'll dine in an hour. Leah will care for Ana while we discuss everything.' Massimo dictated the agenda as if this were merely another business deal.

No doubt Leah was completely capable, but Carrie didn't want her caring for Ana round the clock. But she couldn't say anything until she had herself under control. And it wasn't just anxiety and anger causing her problems.

Every time she looked at Massimo she was hurtled back to that best night of her life. It didn't seem to matter that he'd broken her heart. That he'd disappointed her with his coolness towards their daughter. Carrie's body simply still craved his.

That chemistry was, in fact, stronger than ever. Surely it was just hormones? Maybe it was also some prehistoric instinct to be attracted to the father of her baby—to thirst for his attention because her inner cave woman sought security.

Her brain fought back. She'd figure out her future and that of her daughter's without succumbing to the seductive spell he cast without even knowing—let alone wanting to.

'Am I a prisoner here?' she called as he reached the deck.

He paused and glanced back. Time stretched as his gaze pinned her for too long. 'No.'

The upward inflexion of his smouldering answer sounded more challenging than reassuring. Because how, exactly, would she get off this island? It was accessible only by helicopter or boat. The pilots of both were on Massimo's payroll. As were all the others comprising the 'skeleton staff'. Her joke about emailing an SOS suddenly wasn't that funny.

'So, if I wanted to leave, you'd summon the helicopter?' she pressed.

'Of course.' His sudden smile was arrogantly smug. 'You can leave any time you like.'

There was a pregnant pause before she realised.

'But not Ana,' she said huskily.

He walked out without replying.

Shortly after Leah returned, and Carrie forced

herself to focus on finding out about the woman. It didn't take long for her to feel more relaxed about leaving Ana in her care, at least for a little while. She was insanely well-qualified but, more importantly, she was *kind*.

As Carrie sat in the rocking chair to nurse Ana, she gazed from her daughter to the view. From here she could see there was gym equipment set up on the farthest side of the pool, on the edge of the beach. Massimo now walked towards it, clad only in shorts. Moments later he hung suspended from the high bar. His skin glinted in the late-afternoon sun, his muscles rippling as he performed slow, super-controlled pull-up after pull-up—his strength was staggering.

This was the more urgent matter? He'd chosen to do some exercise instead of holding his child for the first time.

She ignored the unwelcome heat igniting within and raged. The selfishness of him! He was too used to having his own way. Was that the real reason for his insistence that she and Ana stay with him now? Was he playing with their lives in a fit of self-centred, controlling *petulance*? She stared, stunned as he worked out with single-minded force.

And she was *furious*.

CHAPTER EIGHT

I'VE NEVER DONE this before. Any of this.

It didn't matter how hard he pushed himself Massimo couldn't burn enough energy, couldn't slough the heat trapped beneath his skin, couldn't escape the memories that tortured him more than ever. He strode from the sand up the stairs to his own villa and stalked straight into the shower, desperate to forget.

He couldn't.

Who knew why their chemistry was so strong? He'd dated more conventionally beautiful women—svelte models, sparkling graduates, society princesses. He'd never wanted any of them the way he'd wanted her. The way he *still* wanted her. At the time he'd been arrogant enough to think *he'd* been treating *her*, but the gift had been his and he'd devoured it. When he'd seen the unknown number flash up on his phone about a month later, he'd answered it immediately. He'd been delighted she'd finally reached out because he'd been so close to breaking down his own resistance and returning to Auckland to see her.

Her tear-stained face and taut anxiety had pierced through the screen, heralding her most unwelcome news. *Pregnant?* He hadn't just flinched, he'd been so repelled he'd outright rejected her claim. Because he'd been careful. He was always careful. Because it was the last thing he ever wanted. She'd not just seen all that horror, she'd borne the brunt of his anger because he'd lashed out. Scornfully accusing her of...

Guilt made him gag. Had his rude treatment of her impacted on what had happened that night? Had she started bleeding because she'd been so upset, because of *him*? He'd lived with that sickening suspicion for months. And for her not to have got in touch with him since the baby's birth was impossible not to take personally.

Today her doctor hadn't offered many details but had given him a very clear steer that Carrie had suffered a lot in Ana's delivery. That she'd taken a long time to regain strength. That she needed care and rest now.

Massimo's anger billowed. All this trauma could and *should* have been avoided. If she hadn't run away, he could have helped her. She could've had medical care and known the pregnancy had held. He could have flown family over for her if she'd wanted him to. He still could, if she wanted. If she trusted him enough even to *tell* him about her family.

But he couldn't blame her for not doing so. He'd let her down.

After his own lonely childhood and the betrayal he'd suffered in his teens, he didn't want emotional encumbrance. Life was more *efficient* and easier without it. He liked his work and the liberty of his solo lifestyle. He'd never wanted the responsibility of someone else's happiness. His father had loved his mother too much. Had wanted too much. Had expected too much. So had she. And people lied, they let one another down, they left—all that was inevitable.

Honestly, he'd been happy—fantastic, in fact— since his life had been stripped of familial duty. He'd taken pleasure in the pursuit of business success, in the physical satisfaction of sex…and little else. He didn't *need* anything else. Only now that duty had roared right back in on an unstoppable freight train—in the form of a strawberry-blonde and her sweet-cheeked, green-eyed baby. A baby he could scarcely bear to look at. She was too small. Too perfect.

And her mother?

The cold shower did nothing to ease his anger or the thrum of frustration coursing through his hot blood. Carrie was the whole reason he'd come to Fiji in the first place of course. She'd put the idea in his head with her passionate argument for paradisiacal beach holidays, and her smart-mouthed suggestion he might find a suitable sustainability project to support here…for the future of those children he'd sworn he'd never have.

The joke was on him. But he had it together now, right? His plan had been perfectly executed and he had everything exactly as he wanted—both her and the baby safe and secure on this island. Now they could work it all out.

Her astonishment over his purchase of the island, the way she'd queried her ability to leave… Had he wanted to punish her? Imprison her? Exert his control?

Yes. He'd wanted to assuage the outrage of her secrecy. He'd wanted to flex his power. He still did. He had to keep a close eye on her and he refused to feel guilty about coercing her into coming with him today. She didn't appear to have any sort of plan. The irresponsibility of her decisions appalled him. It was time she learned running away didn't work.

But that cold shower still hadn't done its job.

How could he still want her when she'd hidden so much from him? He buttoned his shirt wrong. He ripped it off and slid on a tee shirt. He walked down to the dining deck to the stunning view and complete privacy he'd requested. At least here she couldn't avoid the conversations they needed to have.

He gritted his teeth as she walked towards him. She still wore the teal dress and white canvas shoes. She was still stunning. Basic instinct, wasn't it—and basic stupidity—to want more of the forbidden? Like a child being told he couldn't have any more sweets, he only wanted to scoff every last one. That was what denial did—made him unable to think of anything else. Made him addicted. Made him *obsessed*.

And *that* was where he drew the line. Because he was not going to give way to such a destructive inclination. His father's obsessive love had ultimately led to Massimo's abandonment. Massimo wasn't doing that to his baby. He was damn well going to stay in control, compromise and come to a perfectly satisfactory solution that they could both tolerate. He'd keep both Ana and Carrie safe and secure.

'Does Leah have everything in hand in the

nursery?' he asked when it became evident she wasn't about to offer polite chit-chat.

'For the moment.' Her features tightened as she served some aromatic spiced fish onto her plate. 'What do you want to do?' she asked, not picking up her fork to eat. 'I'm figuring that you've organised all this already, so no doubt your plans go much further.'

'We get married.'

'You don't want children.' She barely skipped a beat. 'I'm quite sure you don't want a wife either.'

He sipped his drink, needing a moment to recalibrate. There was a lot she didn't know about him.

'You were appalled,' she added softly. 'You know you were.'

'I was shocked,' he said stiffly, not controlled enough to explain his deeply personal pain right now. 'I was careful. I've never had such an incident before.' But he hadn't been as careful as usual, either. He'd been desperate and he'd relied on condoms that might've been a century old, for all he knew. 'I was more experienced,' he conceded. 'I let you down. I apologise for that.'

Her blue gaze was frank. 'It wasn't either of our faults,' she said. 'And Ana is here now.'

'Yes.' He gritted his teeth. 'So, we marry.'

She actually rolled her eyes. 'That's not necessary.'

'You don't think?'

'This isn't Victorian England. A myriad of diverse relationships is accepted now. There's no stigma about having a child out of wedlock.'

'Perhaps, but there are still valid—I'd say *vital*—reasons requiring us to marry.'

She stiffened.

'Don't get me wrong,' he muttered. 'I don't actually want to marry you either. This is far from ideal.' He'd *never* wanted to marry but he'd do this because he had to. Because it wouldn't be a traditional type of marriage anyway. 'But I'll put up with it for the sake of the baby. You can too. Or don't you want to do what's best?'

Her blue eyes sharpened. 'I don't think that our being married is in any way best for *Ana*.'

Carrie hadn't left enough time to change or even check out her own accommodation before hurrying to dinner. She'd been too busy being furious with him and then tending to Ana. Now he looked appallingly handsome in that fresh tee and trousers. She had to avoid looking at him but, looking around her, she couldn't cope with the sheer romance of the environment. Everything was geared towards luxurious intimacy. The crisp linen-clad dining table stood on a secluded private deck. The view stretched beyond the leafy grounds to the pale golden sands and endless ombre-blue waters. In the far distance, other islands rose from the shades of blue, while the evening sky was scalded in pinks and golds as the sun began to set.

It was the kind of thing conjured by Hollywood—a perfect island paradise. In an alternative reality, she would have adored it. A reality in which she hadn't just been confronted by the most grim wedding proposal ever. It wasn't even a proposal. It was an order.

'What is best for her, then, in your opinion?' he prompted, forcing her to face him again.

'We could go…' She trailed off, partially lost in those green eyes.

Fiji wasn't practical for him businesswise. New Zealand was neither her home nor his. She'd never been to Australia. She had no family there, no friends. But it was *his* home, and where his business was. She didn't even have a permanent job. So the answer was obvious.

'You have no plans to return to England?'

'Not at this stage.'

He took another sip of his wine. The tension in

his jaw eased. Had he thought she was going to flee to the United Kingdom without even getting in touch with him? She regretted her silence more than ever. Truthfully, she'd liked him so much that she hadn't been ready to face him again. Not that she could tell him that *now*. She had to get over herself. Quickly. Lust could be controlled. Fairy-tale fantasy nights could be forgotten.

'Is there no family you want to come and support you?' He rolled his shoulders. 'I'm happy to fly someone else here if you'd like that.'

She inwardly shrivelled.

'Have you *told* your parents?' His frown deepened. 'Are there even parents to tell?'

He knew so little about her and she knew as little about him. They'd had one night—with no confessions, no sense of the commitment that came with confidences.

'My parents live in England,' she said awkwardly. 'I have two sisters there too. I'm the middle child. And, no, I don't want any of them flying out to help save me from my own stupidity.'

'So they don't know?'

She looked at him. 'I couldn't manage to tell *you*. I was hardly about to tell them. Or anyone.'

'Are you ashamed?'

'Not of Ana. Never Ana.' In that sense, Carrie didn't care about anyone any more. Ana was the most precious thing in her life. 'But *how* it happened,' she admitted. 'How *I* didn't know… I understand why people don't believe me. *I* can't believe it of *myself.*'

He watched her. 'Your own family wouldn't believe you?'

She shrugged, swallowing back the self-pity.

'They wouldn't come and help you if you asked them to?' he asked quietly.

'They're very busy. They have big lives.'

'Big, busy lives doing what?' he echoed thoughtfully.

'You've not heard of the Barrett sisters? They're international athletics champions. Maddie is heptathlon, Rosalyn is pole vault.'

'Athletics?' He stared at her.

'They're amazing,' Carrie said, still staunchly supportive despite everything. 'Like, seriously amazing. Very glamorous too. Social media sponsorships and everything. They're just stunning.'

'And your parents?'

'Lawyers. My father was an amateur athletics champion in his day. Maddie is almost finished her law degree now—she's going into the firm part-time while she's still competing.'

'They definitely all sound busy. While you're on the other side of the world, desperately escaping to your Pacific island paradise.'

She *had* moved across to the other side of the world to escape. Yet disappointment clung to her like a damp cloud that wouldn't evaporate no matter how hot the sun. The betrayal of those she'd thought she was closest to still stung.

'Why is that?' he asked when she said nothing. 'What did they do?'

It was more what they *hadn't* done. As a child, they hadn't given her the attention she'd longed for. Even when she'd tried to be someone they needed, it still hadn't been enough. She'd thought she'd found her place with Gabe. But when he'd met her family—the better versions—he'd fallen for Maddie. Her sister, who'd always won everything. The sister Carrie had given up a term of study to support while she'd been competing on the European circuit. Maddie, who felt no guilt about 'falling in love' because 'it just happened'.

Gabe had admitted that he'd grown bored with Carrie anyway. She'd been sidelined completely. And Carrie had just accepted it all. She'd even done that damned reading.

'You should call them,' he said when she didn't answer.

'Maybe later,' she muttered. 'Once we've made a solid plan.'

She glanced up and caught his intent gaze. Time stopped again. Heat twisted as treacherous desire uncoiled in the hum of that wretched chemistry. How could she react to him like this from one look?

'If you don't want their help then would you object to settling in Australia?' he asked huskily. 'You know I can ensure Ana's needs are met. And yours.' He cleared his throat. 'Financially.'

'We still don't need to get married for that.'

She needed to maintain a *practical* perspective. To focus on what was best for Ana. There was no denying Massimo could provide so much that Carrie couldn't. He thought nothing of buying an entire Pacific island paradise, and financial security mattered. But Carrie was determined to be around to provide the *unconditional* love.

'Actually, marriage will strengthen your immigration case,' he said.

A hard ball of self-preservation in her solar plexus propelled her to say no. Not only to protect herself, but her daughter. Ana, who he still hadn't looked at properly. Ana, who needed better.

'If you're the father on Ana's certificate, then her entry ought to be assured,' she said. 'So I can go in on another type of visa.'

'Are you willing to take the risk of rejection?' He paused for effect. 'What if you're denied entry—could you stand there and watch me carry her straight through Customs without you?'

Her stomach dropped. It was a horrifying image. 'That wouldn't happen.'

'Worse things have. Wouldn't it be better to be certain?' he asked softly.

He had her in a corner but she wasn't willing to concede. 'So you're okay for us to lie to achieve certainty?'

'What's the lie?' he challenged. 'We slept together. We have a relationship of sorts. Who's to say a marriage between us isn't legitimate? We can define it however we want. The details are no one else's business.'

'But you don't want to be married to me for long.'

'We'll be married for as long as is necessary.'

'But we wouldn't be sleeping together. We wouldn't be—'

'You don't want to sleep with me again?' he interrupted, a wry smile curving his lips.

Battling the blush slithering across her skin like

an alien contagion, she replied as best she could. 'I think that one night was enough, don't you?'

The infuriating man smirked and her embarrassment morphed into something else. Something hotter and more intense. *Rage, right?*

'Won't you find it difficult to remain celibate the entire time we're married?' he queried.

'Because I've been so sexually active up til now?' she scoffed tartly. 'I won't find it *hard*. How about you?'

His eyes glinted.

'I don't want a succession of other women in Ana's life,' she added determinedly.

'I don't want a series of random men passing through her life either,' he said smoothly. 'But I do want you to get permanent residency so we can all reside in the same country.'

She drew a breath. 'How long does it take to get residency?'

The merest pause. 'I understand it can take three to four years.'

Her jaw dropped. *Years?* 'We have to be married *that* long?'

'I believe so.' He studied her with that smirk hovering. 'Will that be a problem?'

'What do you think?'

She knew he was right about a lot of things. He

was too astute, too well-researched. She wouldn't get a visa any other way—she didn't have some special skill there was a shortage of…she didn't have loads of money to invest in the country. Her only chance was on a partner visa. So she needed to come up with another solution. This was too challenging.

'I need time to think everything through.'

'Take your time, Carrie.' Sitting back, he toyed with the stem of his wine glass. 'This is neutral territory.'

Neutral? Hardly. This was his island. And his terminology showed he viewed this as a kind of war. What did he expect her to surrender? She had a horrible, hot premonition that it was going to be too much.

'We can stay here for as long as you need,' he added, as if he were being nothing but accommodating.

As long as was needed until she said *yes*.

CHAPTER NINE

CARRIE STARED UP at the delicate awning covering her massive bed. She'd been staring at it for the last seven hours. Cocooned in the luxuriously cool cotton sheets, with Ana nearby and a plan of sorts for the immediate future, she *should* have slept peacefully. Instead she'd been tormented by unbidden memories and rekindled desire as inappropriate thoughts circled in a constant agony. So it was a relief when Ana woke early.

Carrie whispered to Leah that she didn't need her help. Fully focusing on her daughter would keep her present and grounded. But as she fed and changed her child she still couldn't shake Massimo from her head. He had literally everything—looks, intellect, ambition and money. Yet, while he'd gone to such lengths in preparing this place, he'd not held Ana, not spoken to her. He'd not asked Carrie about her at dinner, nor come to the nursery to say goodnight. It didn't make sense when he'd basically kidnapped them and brought them to a place from which there was no easy escape.

But she remembered the way he'd looked at Ana in the hospital in the helicopter. Except he'd battened down that emotion—resisting the obvious urge to reach out. Was he determined to stay distanced? If so, why?

Carrie pulled on her blue sundress and, cradling Ana, crossed onto the sand and strolled down to the water. She breathed deep, drawing in the beauty and optimism of the fresh day. Surely they could work out a sustainable solution? She watched the sun slowly bring colour to the vast sky, feeling the water glide back and forth across her feet with the gentle tide.

'Carrie?'

Her pulse skipped. So easily he knocked her equilibrium. She turned and lost her breath. His black board shorts and white tee shirt highlighted his long limbs, his strong, sleek physique. But the second he saw Ana in her arms his expression hardened.

'Shouldn't she go indoors before it gets too hot?' He glanced back to the buildings.

'Her *name* is Ana.'

A flash flood of disappointment toppled her two seconds of serenity. Was this simply about pride and possession—some 'alpha overlord' need to claim ownership and control even when he didn't actually want either of them?

'Is it?' he countered. 'Her birth hasn't been registered yet. She doesn't have a full name, certainly not *mine*. You don't think I would have liked input into that?'

Honestly, to Carrie he didn't appear to want any kind of input into Ana's life. But she swallowed the bitterness down. It was early and his words had unveiled the deep chasm still separating them—anger and mistrust still burned.

She drew a steadying breath and tried to explain. 'You met my friend Sereana yesterday. She helped me through my recovery after the birth. I wanted to honour her.'

Massimo blamed her for the difficulties of Ana's delivery. He'd already argued that, had she faced him so much earlier when she'd thought she'd miscarried, then that frantic confusion would never have happened. He was probably right. But that didn't mean that her choice to honour her friend wasn't valid. She hoped he would understand.

'But I haven't chosen a middle name or anything,' Carrie said softly, trying to meet him halfway, hoping this revealed true interest—not ownership. 'She could take your surname if that's what you want.' Her heart sank at his continued silence. 'Is there a particular name you'd prefer?' Was there someone *he* wished to honour?

He gazed across the azure waters, his jaw tense. He finally glanced at her. 'Ana is a pretty name and it's appropriate to honour your friend. The lawyers will file the registration.'

'Lawyers?'

'I've engaged one on your behalf. You need advice and it needs to be independent of my own.' He pulled his phone from his pocket.

Mere moments after he sent a message, Leah appeared.

'Carrie needs a rest,' he said curtly. 'Please take Ana back to the nursery.'

Carrie didn't need a rest. Further more, she was perfectly capable of taking Ana to the nursery herself. Heaven forbid Massimo should do it.

'You resent Leah?' He misread her frown as she watched Leah carry Ana inside. 'You know if I'd really wanted you out of the picture you would be by now. But I'm not completely without humanity. I know a baby needs a consistent carer.'

She didn't think he was completely without humanity but his term 'consistent carer' was deliberately emotionless.

'You mean her mother?' she clarified dryly. 'Or maybe even her father?'

He shot her a look. 'A baby needs stability and security. Ideally with one primary person. Other people can be introduced over time but they don't have to be the biological parents.'

'Mansplain away, why don't you?' she said tartly. 'But we're *both* here and we can *share* the responsibility for *Ana*'s stability and security. And doesn't it take a village anyway?' She stepped towards him. 'I don't understand you. If you're not all that interested in her why are you bothering to do all—?'

'What makes you think I'm not interested in her?'

'You won't hold her,' Carrie blurted, unable to hold back now. 'You won't spend any time with her. You just sent her indoors within seconds of seeing her—'

'Because I don't want her getting sunburned or overheated. *You* should get indoors too.'

He made it sound as if he was all concern. But he wasn't.

'You know, you could just pay me off completely,' Carrie said. 'I'll take her and care for her on my own. You don't need to develop a conscience if you don't want to.'

'Not happening.' He gritted his teeth. 'I don't trust other people to do important things. Not without my oversight.'

'You don't trust *me* to make important decisions for her?' She would *always* put Ana first.

'Do you blame me for not trusting you yet?' he asked. 'I like to get the job done myself, then I can be sure it has been done.'

'So this is about *control*, not caring!' she snapped. 'You're not interested in *her*. The second you saw that I was holding her, you frowned.'

'I frowned the second I saw your face and how tired *you* still are,' he contradicted fiercely. 'You look like you haven't slept at all.'

Derailed, she stared at him.

'I want the best for our baby,' he said in exasperation. 'Ana needs a mother who's healthy and not looking as if she's about to collapse any second. Rest and recovery *has* to be your priority. You need a break.'

'I don't need a break from *her*.'

She'd not been able to care for Ana in those first days. She'd been so unwell it had taken almost a week for her to return to full consciousness, let alone be *competent*. She still felt guilty about that even when she'd not been at fault.

Now she worried that, if she didn't have time

to forge her importance in her own child's life, she might be easily excised from it. He already had a super nanny in position. And Carrie didn't just want to matter, she *needed* to.

The horrible truth was she'd left her own family back in England and they weren't very bothered. They'd been too busy to notice the gap she'd left. It felt as if all the effort she'd put into supporting them hadn't just been unrecognised but unappreciated. She wanted Ana to feel her mother loved and valued her—utterly.

'This has been far harder on you than it needed to be,' he said. 'You're so pale…you look terrible.'

Massimo gritted his teeth because, while the first was true, the second was a lie. She was stunning and he was working hard to stop his primal reaction to her proximity. But the tightening of his muscles…

'Maybe I just need a little sunshine.' Hurt bloomed in her eyes.

She was the sunshine. He'd been unable to resist coming to the water when he'd seen her in the distance. But, when she'd faced him, the drawn look in her face had concerned him. Now he regretted saying anything because she looked even more pale.

His fault. Again. Because, truthfully, this was

all his fault. He'd barely slept as he'd considered what she'd been through, and what the doctor had told him yesterday—cautioning him to take care of her. And taking care of her didn't mean tumbling her to the sand and kissing every inch of her gorgeously soft skin.

As she tilted her face towards the sky he couldn't stop staring, could barely resist the desire to reach out and touch. He drew a breath. The last thing she needed was him complicating matters with his unresolved urges. As for her questioning his interest in Ana? That hurt. Because she was right. She'd seen through to his limitations.

Intensity ruined lives. Love, he'd learned from his father, was all-consuming and ultimately destructive. Massimo knew he shared some traits with the man—intense focus, for one thing. So he turned his obsessiveness to work instead. While there was physical release in sex, he'd never allow an emotional connection to form—not one that might over-power everything else. But he couldn't abandon Ana—emotionally or otherwise. He wasn't going to let history repeat itself. He knew too intensely how much it hurt a child. It had devastated him. Which meant he had to find some kind of middle ground.

'Look, we both know I didn't want children, but now Ana's here and I want the best for her.' He tried to explain. 'I want her to know who her family is. I want her to know where and how she belongs in this world. She deserves to have that knowledge and security.'

Because he'd not had it. He'd had only secrets and ultimately betrayal. He wasn't having Ana suffer that. So, not only did he understand Carrie's desire to name Ana in tribute to her friend, he respected it.

The curiosity in Carrie's gaze was impossible to deny.

'Surprises in the family aren't great,' he added reluctantly. 'Ana should know who both her parents are. Where she fits in. She should understand her places and her people.'

The fact that Carrie hadn't told anyone in her family yet concerned him. That she thought they wouldn't believe her and wouldn't want to help her. That made his skin tighten. Because Carrie wasn't like him—she wasn't hardened, independent and tough—she was kind and sweet and she should have better support than that. Didn't her family see that in her?

'But she needs to know *you*, not just who you are,' Carrie said. 'Doesn't that mean *you* need to spend time with her and not just send her inside with the nanny?'

He clenched his jaw, annoyed that his actions had been so misinterpreted. 'That nanny is vital. I don't want you to be overwhelmed or isolated. I'm trying to do the right thing for *you* too. And, for what it's worth, I had a great nanny.'

Her eyes widened. 'You did?'

'Yes. She was lovely.'

She'd been Massimo's only support until he'd turned seven and been sent away to boarding school. He'd been so naïve, he'd thought she'd be waiting for him in the holidays, but he'd never seen her again. His father had dismissed her as an unnecessary expense now he'd been school age—not understanding Massimo's needs at all. Not understanding his devastation. Certainly not caring.

'Frankly, I haven't had time to adjust to the concept of fatherhood myself,' he admitted huskily.

'I didn't get time to adjust either,' Carrie tossed back. 'She just arrived and I had to get on with it as soon as I was well enough. For *her*. *She* is the priority.'

'I know that.' His tension built. 'But I have no idea—'

'And you think I did?' Carrie said quietly. 'Just *start*. Spend time with her, not money. Get better from there.'

He hated that she was schooling him. That she was right—in part. But she didn't understand where he was coming from and he had no intention of discussing anything so deeply *personal*. The truth was, he wasn't supposed to have been born at all. His parents had been unable to conceive and in the end his mother had secretly gone with an alternative. Massimo had learned years later that said alternative was a serial cheater who'd taken advantage of his mother's desperation. Who'd never actually been interested in being a *dad*.

Massimo's actual father hadn't been interested either. He'd only agreed to try for his wife's sake and after her death he'd barely engaged with Massimo—apparently too bereaved to cope. Years later, when he'd found out the truth, it had enabled him to do what he'd always wanted— abandon Massimo completely.

'Now that we're here, I can do exactly that,' he said stiffly, pushing back on the memories. 'But let's agree we operate with wildly different expectations. I expected you to be in touch with me sooner. You expect more from me as a father.

Perhaps we both need to make adjustments.' He sighed. 'Fighting isn't going to make this easier. We need to give each other a chance to catch a breath.'

Carrie stared at Massimo. Catching her breath around him was an impossible ask. But he was offering an olive branch and they were aligned in wanting the best for Ana. He wanted her to be well, and she appreciated that.

Maybe she'd been impatient with him because of her own family baggage. He didn't know anything about that. And, given he'd been raised by a nanny, maybe there were other things she didn't know. Maybe he had issues of his own to work through.

'Okay.'

'Okay.' He smiled at her.

Carrie's skin tingled. When he smiled like that his eyes lit up—making their striking colour even more contrasting. It made her want to smile back. To lean in. To let him…

No.

It would be like deliberately throwing herself into a fire. And if she succumbed to this weakness she might lose control not just of her heart, but of what would happen with her daughter. She had to put Ana first.

'You know, we don't need to stay here all that long, do we?' She fidgeted. 'I mean, we agree that we both want what's best for Ana, so we could just go to Australia now. We don't need to stay here to figure out the finer details.' She worried her lower lip when he didn't respond. 'I know you've gone to all this trouble…'

'Indeed I have,' he said softly. 'What is it about the place that you don't like?'

'Nothing. It's beautiful. But—'

'Then why not rest here for a few more days?' He stepped closer. 'You *are* tired. The doctor said…'

'Said what?' She stilled, defensiveness flaring.

'That you'd been through a lot. And you need rest.'

Great, so he was being nice to her on doctor's orders. She'd misread the concern in his eyes for something else. It was mortifying.

'When we head to Sydney, it might get a little busy,' he said. 'People will be interested in you.'

'No, they won't.'

His eyes narrowed slightly. 'I'm wealthy. There-fore, stupid as it is, they'll want to know who you are. Especially when we arrive with a baby.'

They were going take one look at her and know

he was only with her *because* of the baby. 'They don't scare me.' She shrugged, defiantly refusing to care any more about what others thought of her and about not living up to anyone's expectations or immediately failing.

'No? People don't scare you?' he jeered softly. 'Someone who's dreamed her whole life about escaping to a remote paradise island to read books on the beach?'

She stared at him. 'If they want to know, then maybe we should go face them and get it over with.'

'Are you scared to be alone here with *me*?'

She shot him a look. 'You're still unbelievably arrogant.'

'Doesn't mean I'm not right.' He gazed into her eyes. 'You know you scare me.'

'No, *chemistry* scared you. But that's long gone.'

He stilled before abruptly turning towards the building. 'Well, what scares me most right now is seeing you sunburned. At least put on some sunscreen.'

As she walked with him towards the deck outside her suite of rooms, he glanced at her dress. 'Didn't any of the clothes suit?'

She shot him a mystified look. 'What clothes?'

'I had supplies for you delivered. Haven't you looked at them?' He stepped inside to her bedroom and went to the cupboard next to the bathroom. Except it wasn't a cupboard. It was a whole other room, and on the long garment racks hung dresses, skirts, blouses and casual tee shirts, even shoes still in boxes, neatly stacked. Who needed shoes when the sand outside was so fine it was like walking on talcum powder?

'I didn't look in here last night. I was busy with Ana.' Now she stared in amazement at the display. 'Did you order all this?'

'The standard selection, sure.'

She eyed him warily. 'This is the "standard selection"?'

'The department store's standard selection.' He nodded carelessly. 'That's what the assistant said she'd pull together. A capsule wardrobe or something?'

This wasn't a capsule. This was colossal. And of course he'd not *personally* selected every item—Carrie mocked herself for the half-second she'd thought he had. He'd simply given a personal shopper his credit card details and told her to get on to it. The woman had probably had a ball. She'd certainly done a good job. There was everything Carrie could think of and then so much more as well—even swimsuits.

Carrie opened another drawer and discovered pretty silk and lace. She quickly shut it. 'I can't accept all this.'

'Well, it's here if you want it, or you can keep wearing your favourite sundress twenty-four-seven.' He shrugged.

She knew money wasn't a big deal to him but it was to her. And accepting this didn't feel quite right. She didn't want to *owe* him.

'There's a beauty room you're more than welcome to use,' he added negligently. 'Leah will summon the staff. Just ask her.'

Carrie couldn't cope. 'Are beauticians classed as skeleton staff?'

'Actually, yes,' he said. 'I didn't want any of the resort workers to be made redundant when I took over the complex, even though we're not having paying guests for the foreseeable future.'

She swallowed. 'I don't know what to say,' she muttered. 'This is all…'

'Just stuff.' He nodded. 'Enjoy it. Rest. Feel better. Meanwhile I'm going to—'

'Attend to a more important matter?' she asked tartly before thinking better of it. 'Out by the pool?'

His fallen-angel eyes suddenly gleamed and that sinful smile flashed. 'Perhaps. Why? Do you enjoy watching?'

CHAPTER TEN

CARRIE TURNED HER back on his soft laughter and walked to the nursery. She *refused* to watch him working out again. She'd play with Ana. But Ana was currently sleeping soundly in her cot.

'She's just gone down.' Leah glanced up from her crossword puzzle. 'She should sleep for a while yet.'

Carrie nodded as she stared down, melting at the cherubic beauty of her baby sleeping. But after a while the temptation for some self-care sneaked in. A massage…? Besides, she justified, it would be a way of *not* watching Massimo.

'Massimo said there were some staff on the island for the beauty room?'

Leah set aside her crossword and smiled. 'Oh, there is. Give me a couple of minutes.'

Ten minutes later Carrie was blinking hard to believe she was standing in such a stunning space. The beauty room was in a small villa further along the beach. There was a large, deep spa bath on the deck that had views of the water, while inside there were polished wooden floors. Sheer fabrics wafted in the breeze generated by smoothly whirring ceiling fans. Fresh-cut flowers floated in gorgeous water bowls and a gorgeous scent filled the air.

'Would you like a massage first?' asked Naomi, the beautician, anticipation gleaming in her eyes. 'Then we can do a mani-pedi, your hair, a facial—'

'In other words, *everything*!' Carrie giggled nervously. 'That sounds amazing. Thank you.'

Awkwardly she changed into the soft robe. She'd only gone to budget walk-in beauty bars before and had never had a *massage*. But Naomi's friendliness soon put her at ease. And, as the woman gently rubbed her back and shoulders, the luscious botanic scent somehow thinned her thoughts until she heard only the sound of the gentle waves. It was warm and calm and everything was safe. *Ana* was safe. Slowly Carrie's eyes closed.

'Bula Carrie?'

Carrie drowsily blinked at the soft greeting, confused by the colour of the sheer curtains floating in the balmy breeze. Where was she? More to the point, *where was Ana*?

It was Naomi who'd gently roused her and who answered her unspoken question now. 'Leah is just bringing Ana and I have some refreshment for you.'

'Oh, I'm so sorry.' Carrie sat up. 'How long have I been asleep?'

Naomi just laughed. 'You need rest. Don't move, we'll bring everything to you.' She smiled at her. 'New mothers need to be cared for.'

Leah arrived with Ana and Carrie fed her. Refreshed from the nap, she talked to the two women and together they cooed over Ana. Then Leah took her for a walk while Naomi got to work on Carrie with a facial, manicure and on her hair.

Carrie melted. It was *luxurious*. Every inch of her body was cleansed, massaged and cared for. Blissfully indulging herself, she chatted with Naomi, learning about her family, her ambitions and her pleasure in Massimo's plans for the resort.

Two hours later she stared in amazement at her reflection. Her hair had been trimmed and was shining. Somehow the circles beneath her eyes had faded and her skin glowed even though she wasn't even wearing any make-up.

'I brought over one of the dresses from your

room.' Naomi winked at her in the mirror. 'There are some lovely things in there.'

Carrie looked doubtfully at the pale lemon dress Naomi had selected. It looked clingy but she didn't want to disappoint the woman who'd done so much for her. The silky fabric slithered over her body, so soft it was almost sensual. Again she blinked at her reflection. Both the style and colour looked better than she'd imagined they would. She slid her feet into the sleek sandals Naomi produced with a flourish.

'Much better.' Naomi positively beamed.

For a tiny moment Carrie hesitated, but it would be a shame for the clothing to remain unworn. Could she trust his motives? Was she a prisoner in a gilded cage or was he simply demonstrating how comfortable he could make her life to convince her to say yes?

You're not the reason why he brought you here.

He was doing all this for *Ana*. And Carrie couldn't be dependent on him for *everything*. She would need her own space away from him to continue to develop her own sense of self-worth—that was why she'd come travelling in the first place, wasn't it?

She couldn't risk losing her identity and drowning in his, and that was a very real possibility, because his was that forceful. *He* loomed that large in life. Yet she felt more alive than she'd felt in months. And that was him too, wasn't it? Something within her sparked into life when he was around. That first night, she'd laughed and teased easily and had been frankly fearless in what she'd said. Now he provoked her again.

Mulling over her confusing thoughts, Carrie went to see Ana. As she quietly walked onto the deck of the nursery wing she saw Massimo standing beside her cot. Carrie immediately froze, not wanting to intrude. But she wasn't able to look away either. He was only in swimming shorts. But his physical magnificence wasn't what arrested her. It was that *expression*. Still and silent, he gazed down intently at their baby. Fascination, curiosity and wariness flickered across his face—all the feelings that perfectly echoed her own. Ana was so tiny, so perfect, and it was *terrifying* to have complete responsibility for someone so precious.

She didn't want to spoil his private moment but, as she gingerly stepped backwards, he glanced up. She froze, ensnared anew. Because now, having seen her, his green eyes were stormy—gleaming with defiance and a defensiveness she didn't understand.

* * *

Every one of Massimo's muscles screamed with the restraint he exerted over them. He would *not* stride over to her. He would *not* pull her into his arms. He would *not* kiss her. She'd barely recovered from major surgery and he was not going to pounce on her with uncontrolled passion. Leaving her this morning had been hard enough, but *now*?

Now he was overwhelmed with feelings for the tiny creature who'd been gazing up at him every bit as intently as he'd been gazing at her. *Now* he'd glanced up and caught sight of the beautiful woman who'd brought that baby into this world. All he wanted was to bury everything exploding inside him, to blow away this cascade of all-encompassing emotion in the fiery oblivion of sex. He'd take Carrie. *Now.* Get physical. Feel better. Forget.

As if that was going to work! It wasn't how it had worked between them all those months ago and it sure as hell wasn't an option now. He wouldn't use her like that. And he wouldn't give in to that damned overwhelming *temptation*. He would get himself under control.

His muscles howled. He'd just worked out— again—desperate to ease their frenetic twitch.

The whole thing had been a waste of time. He'd been drawn to see Ana because Carrie was right—he'd been avoiding their baby. He'd thought he could sneak in and out, but he'd been standing here for the last twenty minutes, barely coping with the ache consuming him. Ana was so very, very sweet, he could scarcely breathe. She was too small. Too fragile. Frankly he still couldn't believe she was even *real*. He had no damned idea how he was supposed to interact with her. As for *holding* her? He'd break her, right? And he'd be lost.

Who was he kidding? He was already lost, a hostage to fate and fortune. What impacted Ana, impacted him. She was his child, so precious, so vulnerable, he was terrified even to touch her. He didn't have a damned clue how to. He needed an immediate software update—the fatherhood download. Because he felt the burden of responsibility, the fear of failing her, when he knew *nothing*.

Yesterday he'd desperately tried not to notice the natural way Carrie cared for her. It felt intrusive, too intimate to watch. He'd been unable to look away and still couldn't. But his paralysis wasn't for lack of want, it was for lack of *skill*.

He'd thought he ought to stay in his own lane, play to his own strengths...but Carrie had called him out on that. She'd pushed him to do better. And he *wanted* to do better. Only now she'd caught him—frozen. Frankly, useless. Now he couldn't stare at Ana any more because he was staring at Carrie instead. That was worse. And impossible to stop.

His pulse roared. Her hair framed her face, loose and glossy, the strawberry strands gleaming. Her crushed-rosebud-coloured lips looked pillowy. There'd always been a softness to her that he was unable to resist—not then and not now.

'You look lovely,' he croaked.

She brushed her hand down the side of her dress. 'It's amazing what a beauty treatment will do.'

'It's not the treatment.' There was a glow within her that wasn't superficial.

An adorably sheepish pink mottled her cheeks. 'I fell asleep.'

That admission soothed him a little. 'That's good.'

She needed rest. He knew she'd had fantastic care, that those people had done everything possible and more to ensure her wellbeing. But he was still angry. Still guilty. His heart pounded harder because now he had to confront the feelings. The fears. Escaping into sex wasn't an option. 'You lost a lot of blood.'

He chilled, remembering the time years ago when he'd lost blood. It hadn't been life threatening, but it had spilled a terrible secret of its own.

'I'm better. Everything's healed pretty well now.' A hint of embarrassment shimmered in her eyes.

The doctor had crisply informed him yesterday that 'marital relations' could resume. With care. That she could swim. With care. That she'd be fine. With care. Care that Massimo wasn't sure he was capable of.

Carrie walked to the other side of Ana's cot and looked down at the gently stirring baby.

'She has your eyes.' There was a catch in her voice.

'Not my eyes,' Massimo muttered huskily, glancing across the cot to explain to Carrie. 'My mother's.'

'Oh.'

His were the eyes that reminded his father of his loss, his heartache—and because of that he could hardly bear to look at Massimo at all. He'd never let Massimo forget that he'd lost the love of his life because of *him*. She'd made the ultimate sacrifice and Massimo had tried so hard to be worthy of it, naively hoping he might help his father heal…

He never had. And when that final terrible truth had emerged… Massimo had told no one the true circumstances surrounding his conception or the impact of that devastating discovery years later. But this once he felt pressure to explain a little. Carrie ought to understand why he'd reacted as strongly as he had to the chaotic circumstances of Ana's birth and something about why he didn't want children. He wanted her to know he wasn't a total monster.

Carrie was guileless and sweet and the disappointment in her eyes as she'd accused him of being uninterested in Ana had scalded him more than anything his father had screamed at him in the past.

'She died just after giving birth to me.' He forced the basics out.

Her eyes widened. 'I'm so sorry.'

Her words were awash with sympathy he didn't want, and he knew she was waiting for him to tell her more, but he couldn't do details. Not on this.

'I never wanted to put anyone in the position of…' He shrugged.

'*That's* why you don't want children?' Those rosebud lips parted. 'Childbirth worries you?'

It didn't just worry him, it terrified him. 'Utterly. With good reason.'

She swallowed. 'But I'm okay. Truly.'

Was she?

He glanced down at Ana again. 'I never had a mother. And I have no idea how to be a father.'

'You're not close to your own?'

'Never really have been.' His father had been too mired in grief to see him for years, then twisted by bitterness and blame—until one final betrayal had led to absolute abandonment.

'I'm sorry to hear that too.' She hesitated. 'But then I guess you might know a few things *not* to do,' she muttered cautiously. 'That's how I'm trying to work it—not to do some of the things my parents did.'

His curiosity spiked. Despite himself, he had the deep desire to know more about her. 'Such as?'

That sheepish colour mottled her cheeks again. 'I know I've already made mistakes and I'm sure I'll make more.' She shot him a small, wary smile. 'But I'm going to make sure she knows how loved she is. I'm going to tell her and show her. Every single day, so she's never in doubt…'

Carrie was aware Massimo was regarding her even more intently than usual. She ached to know the details she had no right to ask. He'd lost so much—no mother to cradle him, not close to his father. He'd mentioned that nanny… No wonder he'd been angry that Carrie hadn't seen a doctor, that she hadn't been prepared for the birth. That would have made him horribly anxious even after the fact. He wouldn't want his daughter suffering in the way that he had by losing a parent so young…and knowledge was power, wasn't it? Knowledge gave assurance, control. So for him to have been shut out of all information…

'I should have phoned you,' she muttered. 'I promised myself I would but then the days just—'

'It's okay, Carrie,' he interrupted in a low voice. 'The sheer shock, all those emotions and hormones… I understand. And I believe you about not knowing. About everything.'

At the clear ring of forgiveness, she felt hot tears sting her eyes.

'And I am really very sorry about how I reacted when you called me to tell me you were pregnant.' A stricken expression tightened his face. 'I worried that I upset you so much that…'

'You thought it caused my mistaken miscarriage?' She shook her head vehemently. 'No. *No*.'

Suddenly she saw the guilt in *his* eyes, the horror, and her heart tore. His mother had died giving birth to him and then he'd worried all that time that somehow he'd been responsible for her miscarrying his child. That had been a terrible thing to bear.

'No. The doctor here said it's common for some women to get spotting all through their pregnancies. Ana was a healthy weight. It was just how it was for me. And I just thought that it was erratic. It wasn't anything you did. Or that I did. When I went into labour, Ana was the wrong way round so the only way she could get out was with a caesarean. My haemorrhage was just bad luck.'

He gazed at her, swallowing, as if it were hard to speak. 'I'm still sorry.'

'So am I,' she whispered. 'Because you were right, I should have seen a doctor so much sooner. But I think we need to put that all behind us now.'

Another long pause.

'Just like that?'

She drew in a breath and braved it. 'Yes?'

The tension in his eyes slowly ebbed and he smiled. And *just like that* she was seduced again and hope blossomed. Maybe this *was* going to be okay. Maybe this was going to...

Ana mewled. Both Carrie and Massimo startled.

'She'll be hungry.' Carrie quickly stepped away from the cot so that Massimo could stay. 'I wasn't well enough to feed her myself at first so I supplement with a bottle.'

Massimo didn't pick Ana up but he did place a gentle hand on her stomach while Carrie checked the bottle that Leah had left ready.

Carrie breathed though the twisting pull of hope and fear of rejection. 'Do you want to feed her?' Her offer was belated, awkward, possibly unwanted.

His lips twisted. 'I might watch and learn this time.'

Carrie nodded. Compromise could work, couldn't it?

'I didn't know what I was doing.' She sat with Ana in the rocking chair, babbling to ease her own tension. 'I watched the nurses. But new and difficult things get easier with practice, right? I've always had to practise things a lot.'

'Oh? I thought you were a fast learner.'

There was a teasing lightness in his tone and she knew he intended to remind her of that night.

She glanced at him balefully. It wasn't fair of him to switch into that charming man again. Not when she'd finally thought they might be *friends*.

'You know, there's a wide spectrum between failing and excelling.' He sat in the chair Leah had used earlier. 'There's doing okay. Good enough.'

'You don't really believe that.' She half-laughed. 'I bet you've never failed at anything.'

His eyebrows shot up. 'That's flattering but completely wrong. Though you're right about practice,' he added softly. 'It builds confidence.'

She glanced at him askance. Had she misheard that *suggestion* in his tone? He didn't think she ought to practice *that*, again, did he?

Amusement suddenly danced in his eyes but his tone switched back to bland. 'When I first went into business, I had no idea what I was doing. I couldn't believe people were asking me to invest their life savings for them.'

She couldn't imagine him suffering doubts. 'Did you make the right calls?'

'Mostly. Miraculously, none of my mistakes were too massive. The more decisions I made, the better I got at making them. Although…' he suddenly looked impish '… I wonder if I might be too used to making decisions *unilaterally*.'

'Autocratic, you mean? Dictatorial?' She smiled, enjoying the easy tumble back into banter. 'I guess you're used to having to. When you're the boss, you're the one people look to for answers.' She lifted her chin and reminded him. 'But, Massimo, you're not the boss of *me*.'

'Apparently not.' That amused glint in his eye was now laced with challenge.

The tension between them changed. Antagonism melted as attraction resurged. The chains she'd desperately locked around her desire inside loosened. They might just have made a tentative peace but now she realised her true problems had just proliferated.

CHAPTER ELEVEN

NOT BEING IN CHARGE. Not being in control—of himself and of everything? Yeah. Massimo wasn't used to it. But he hadn't spent most of his life overcoming expectations and challenges to abandon the attempt now. Carrie had set him a challenge and he'd meet it. He'd learn how to handle Ana.

He'd *also* learn to handle his own urges which were worsening by the hour. The desire to seduce Carrie was so wrong. She'd been through the wringer and they had too much to work out for him to wreck the situation any more with something as weak as lust. Except that was the problem. This lust wasn't weak. It was overpowering his *reason*. And that was alarming.

He needed structure. A timetable. He worked out and then worked remotely, taking meetings online late into the evening. He kept up with business well enough. But he was distracted.

He spent time with Ana. He worked alongside Leah, determined to master at least the basics.

But he couldn't control his hyper-awareness of Carrie. He watched her in the distance as she paddled along the shoreline, fighting the urge to follow her, to lean close and breathe in her scent, to touch her silky skin and press into her sweet softness.

He lay awake hours into the night, reminding himself why he had to keep his distance. She was still physically vulnerable. And what little she'd told him about her family was an additional warning—she wanted to ensure Ana was loved. Valued. The inference was easy to make. Carrie hadn't felt that. Which made her more emotionally vulnerable than he'd realised. He couldn't give her the kind of romance or love he suspected she craved. But he *needed* her to marry him. He needed to solidify her immigration status and create that security for Ana.

Confusing her with no-holds-barred sex? *Not an option*. But it took everything in him to resist.

Carrie discovered Massimo's paradise island *was* still a prison, just a different kind. Where she should be relaxed, she felt nothing but restrained, unable to act on the desires eating her up inside. Inappropriate. *Unwanted.*

She *should* be happy, right? She should feel

upbeat and positive, excited even, that she and Massimo had resolved some things and now had a basis upon which to move forward. But a powerful instinct still held her back from saying yes to marriage.

They'd been on the island another two nights and, while they'd settled into a regular routine, her base level anxiety hadn't lowered. Instead it was steadily rising and she was plagued by restlessness. Resisting the urges of her own body, enduring the ache not just for his touch but his *time*, was a slow torture—watching him in the distance, maintaining polite conversation every evening at dinner.

Get a grip.

Right now he was down on the beach and Carrie was *not* reading the novel she had open on her knee. He'd just done some massive workout in the gym and then Leah had brought Ana over to him. Watching him take the baby so carefully, the size of Ana in his muscled arms, seeing him relaxed, unguarded and laughing... The way he looked at Ana, his expression unreserved and open, frankly adoring.

A knot tightened inside. Was she actually jealous of her beautiful little baby?

His torso was tanned and gleaming and his

muscles primed. Carrie was primed too. Just watching him had her horrifically aroused and aching for the press of his body. But worse than the chemistry was the mushiness of her heart. The scarred protective layer had been stripped by the sight of him showering Ana with his attention. Raw lust was slowly transforming into something scarier.

Nope. She was not falling for him. She refused.

She'd not given in to her longings for him before—she wouldn't now. They were only worse because hormones were at play and she'd been through a tough time. Her feelings for him weren't *real*. But he'd said he believed her. It had been so long since she'd had *anyone* believe in her, and she couldn't tear her gaze away as he carried Ana from the beach to the deck where she waited. Tall and muscled carrying tiny and sweet.

'I can't get used to how little she is,' he murmured. 'She's the most perfect thing.'

'On the planet,' Carrie agreed. But Massimo and Ana together? It was the most perfect thing in the universe.

'Time disappears,' he added. 'I don't even know where the day drifts.'

Pleasure flooded Carrie. Her baby girl had

wormed her way into his heart and now he was as besotted as she. Her child had a father who would do anything for her. Who would always *adore* her. That flicker of jealousy died completely because she wanted her child to have *everything* she'd never had. Now she was just grateful.

Another day floated by. Never had she felt like such a princess... She didn't have to cook, didn't have to think about work, didn't even have to make her own bed. Except she didn't have to do public appearances, so this was *way* better than being some poor put-upon royal. It was an utterly spoilt, charmed life but it came with a catch—the total threat to her heart.

Massimo was too easy to say yes to. Too impossible to say no to.

Sitting at the table on her deck in the shade, she pulled out her laptop and got to work. Avoidance. Distraction. Helping someone else had to help her too.

'What are you doing?'

She didn't glance up. In her peripheral vision she could see he was in those wretchedly flattering swimming trunks again. And nothing else. Again.

'Spreadsheet,' she muttered.

'You shouldn't be working. You still need to rest.'

'I am resting. While working.' She glanced up at him. 'I'm not an invalid. I had a baby. Weeks ago now.'

'The point of us staying here is for rest and recuperation, but you look more tired than when we first arrived.' Massimo crouched beside her. 'Are you not sleeping?'

The gently asked question made her slide further beneath his spell. She glanced at him and discovered he was too close. She swallowed as his mossy green gaze burned through to her secrets.

'I'm not either.'

She *felt* rather than heard his low admission. The raw, underlying emotions hit hard—lust, but resentment too. Desire so strong but just as strongly unwanted. It was better to stay level-headed, slightly distanced. To focus on Ana and only on Ana. Because Ana was the only reason they were here at all. But her body wasn't listening. Her body just wanted his. His time, his attention, his touch.

'Leah told me we're supposed to sleep when Ana does,' he said. 'Instead, you're working. You're not even reading your novels.' He put his hand on hers. 'You know, you don't owe Sere-ana. She wouldn't expect you to work right now.'

'I do owe her,' Carrie said. 'But that's not the only reason I'm doing this.' She risked a glance at him. 'I *like* what I'm doing.'

'Spreadsheets?'

'Why sound so sceptical? You like figures.'

'True.' He chuckled. 'What's in your spread-sheets?'

Talking about work was less dangerous than playing with innuendo. She could focus on her project, not the fact that he was gorgeous.

'I'm a sports administrator. You know, the one who organises training grounds and the sched-ules for competitions. I work out the progression for the draws, health and safety… It probably sounds boring.'

'No. You got into it because of your sisters?'

'Yeah.' Since she was ten she'd quietly got on with the tasks her family were too busy for. Finding her place—her purpose—had been par-amount. 'My family were all very busy. I wasn't a competitor. I found I was better at organising everything for them. I even took a term off my degree to support Maddie on the European cir-cuit a couple of years ago. She said she desperately needed me, but basically I'm just a really good side-line supporter.'

A small smile flitted into his eyes. 'Who's your side-line supporter?'

She laughed, not going to let him show how her parents' words had hurt. 'I'm not good enough to compete.'

'Not good enough?' His eyebrows lifted.

'They're all about *winning*.'

'So if you're not going to win…?'

'Then you don't race.' She nodded. 'I couldn't please them.'

'You should please only *yourself*, Carrie.'

It wasn't that easy when family was involved. 'Did you never want parental approval?' She stilled, suddenly remembering. He'd lost his mother. Wasn't close to his father. So, maybe not. 'Sorry,' she muttered.

'No, it's okay. I could never get my father's approval. It wouldn't matter what I did.'

Not even when he'd become so successful so young? 'I'm sorry. I know that sucks.'

Massimo's gaze had lowered to her mouth. Now he cleared his throat. 'Why don't we go for a walk? A change of scene might be good.'

'A change of scene?' She laughed. 'You think

you can find a better one?' She gestured towards the beach. 'You can't be bored already?'

'I'm far from bored. That's the problem. Get your walking shoes on. I'll meet you on the beach in ten. Maybe some activity will help us both sleep better.'

He'd said it innocuously enough but she was thinking about the *wrong* kind of activity. Her pulse and mood lifted. They'd not spent much time together. The beach was in full view of the staff and they really only interacted at dinner. That distance had somehow been mutually agreed upon in silence. But they could be friends—if she could ever get her body to agree to the prospect of a platonic relationship.

Fifteen minutes later she followed him along an inland path. Wide leaves of the emerald and jade trees offered shade as they climbed to the highest peak on the perfect patch of paradise. From here they could look down at the resort and she could see the lighter waters of the reef encircling almost all of their island. Other islands dotted the deepening blue in the distance. But it was behind her, just below the summit on the eastern side, that the immediate treasure was found. A tiny, private pool nestled into the rocks.

'Wow...' She gazed at it, stunned. The trees

were so lush they gave the grotto privacy and shelter—from the sun, from sight. 'Even *you* have to admit this is not boring.'

'Not boring at all.' He smiled.

'Admit it, you love a beach holiday. I saw you paddle boarding at dawn this morning,' she added. 'And working out on the gym.'

He waggled his eyebrows. 'Voyeur…'

She caught his eye and blushed. 'Don't let it go to your head. There aren't many other people to watch around here…'

His laugh was low. He whipped his tee over his head.

Carrie gaped. 'What are you doing?'

'Providing you with more visual entertainment.' He shrugged. 'Isn't this better than your spreadsheet?' He waded into the small pool and laughed at her expression. 'I got hot from the walk. Didn't you?'

Not from the walk, she hadn't. But she had a swimsuit on beneath her loose dress and the doctor had given her the all-clear for swimming before she'd left hospital last week. For other more intimate activities too. Not that they were on offer.

She hesitated, increasingly irked by the laughter in his eyes as he floated lazily, frankly showing off his sleek muscles.

'Fine.' She gritted her teeth and slipped her dress off.

The water was just that one degree below perfect, chilled enough to make her shiver yet love it at the same time. It was so lush. It was the second-most pleasurable experience of her life. And it was so, so stunning.

'I've never been anywhere as beautiful as this.'

Massimo waded to the side of the pool and grabbed the thermal-lined bag he'd had slung over his shoulder while they'd walked. To Carrie's delight he pulled out precious, delicious things. Chilled squares of dark chocolate and salted nuts revitalised her. She almost moaned. How could the simplest of things taste so good?

'You were prepared.' She sighed in pleasure.

'I can organise a few things too. And I didn't want you to end up more tired than you already were.'

Carrie froze—both shocked and captivated as he touched her. Slowly he rubbed his thumb against her lip and when he lifted it away she saw a small smear of dark chocolate on his skin. She watched, melting, as he licked it off. They shouldn't. They both knew they shouldn't. But it was like that magical night back in Auckland. The chemistry was too strong and she couldn't resist.

'Massimo,' she whispered.

Whether it was to warn him away or will him closer, she'd never know, because from the first brush of his lips there was no stopping. No slowing. There was just that sizzling arc of electricity that shorted out her reason. She trembled and his answering groan melted any last nugget of doubt. Golden heat radiated beyond her skin—too pure to be contained.

It didn't matter if this was going to complicate things. Her body wasn't interested in the arguments of her rational mind. Her body overruled *everything*. This was too good. He was the one thing she wanted more than anything. And how could it be wrong when they'd made something so wonderful together? The biology between them was perfect, the chemistry completely explosive and the physics elemental—the gravitational pull a force impossible to withstand. As sure as a stone sinking to the bottom of the sea, she would succumb to it.

But she saw the conflict in his eyes as he gazed into hers. He shook his head and she thought he was going to pull away completely. But then he was back, there was a hungrier press of lips and then the sheer, utter delight of his touch. His hands stroked over her swimsuit, touching parts that didn't just ache but burned for him. Shaking uncontrollably, she moaned her need—her utter, desperate, intense need. And he met it, with the most delightful, far too gentle, reverent touch.

And that was all it took. Almost nothing. He caught her scream of ecstasy with his lips. For a moment she felt the heavenly press of him right against her. Only the flimsy barriers of bathing suits separated them.

'No.' He suddenly broke away from her. 'No. This isn't happening.'

Shocked, she blinked. He was out of the water already. She stared at him, bereft. Why had he shut down? Why wouldn't he look at her?

'Massimo?' She was shaking again, but this time on the verge of tears.

'I'm sorry, Carrie. That shouldn't have happened.'

'Um… I wanted it to happen.' Her heart pounded. 'I want more to happen.'

And she *wanted* him inside her. Surely he wanted that too—when *he'd* been the one to instigate it? She'd felt how much he wanted it. Distractedly, he grabbed the chocolate wrapper and shoved it·back in his bag so they'd leave no trace of their presence here.

Her tears evaporated as anger intensified. Why was he so determined to reject what he actually wanted—*her*? He was clearly frustrated but refused to take satisfaction from her. Why had he given it to her, then? Had he just been indulging her? She didn't believe that. She could *see* how much his body wanted her. There was no hiding *that*. So why was he fighting so hard to stop himself from being with her? What did he think was so awful that would happen if he did?

'It's obvious you want me,' she said, shaky but determined. 'Apparently you'd rather sit in a bath of sea snakes than let yourself sleep with me.' She was so hurt. 'What makes me so unworthy?'

'I don't want to hurt you any more than I already have,' he said roughly. 'Hell, Carrie. I took your virginity in a one-night stand. You got pregnant. You then suffered the heartache of a miscarriage, only to discover months later when you went into a crippling labour that you were still pregnant and about to give birth to a slightly premature baby. You lost so much blood, you were lucky to survive. *All* my fault. Every last bit of it.'

'Did I have no say in that night?' she retorted. 'Wasn't I the one who said yes? Wasn't I the one who asked you for several repeats that night? Or was I just some passive creature who lay there and let you do whatever you wanted and make all the decisions? Because that's not how I remember it happening, Massimo.'

A vision of that night swept over her. She'd not been herself. And, even with everything, she'd not regretted it. Not until this very moment when she realised how much *he* regretted it.

He shook his head. 'We need to leave before I do something we both regret.'

'You already regret everything'

'No. I just don't want to hurt you more.' He growled.

'Too late,' she said. 'You just made me feel desperate. Like it was all one-sided. Like I'm the only one who wanted that and you were only *indulging* me.'

It was excruciating. Apparently he could take it or leave it. Whereas she was borderline obsessed. But, though he stood stock-still, his breathing quickened.

'I wasn't *that* prepared,' he said gruffly. 'We can't take the risk of you getting pregnant again.'

Her heart pounded. 'But I…'

He closed his eyes and she trailed off, hurt by the visual rejection. She chose not to tell him she was on the pill now to regulate her crazy periods. Or that she would have caressed him the way he had her... Because he didn't even want that. He was still in control, his release incomplete—and unwanted.

'I don't want you offering yourself to me to assuage any lingering guilt over what happened,' he said.

'That *wasn't* what I was doing.' Embarrassment burned her skin. 'I want you. Or I did, until you started saying stupid things.'

'I have *wrecked* your life, Carrie.'

'I don't see it that way.' She was shocked by the guilt in his tone. 'This hasn't made my life worse. Different, yes. But honestly? Ana has made it so much better.' She looked at him. 'But that's not the same for you. *You're* the one whose life's been wrecked.'

'No.' He shook his head. 'Ana is a gift. But...' He rolled his shoulders uncomfortably. 'We still can't do this. You're too vulnerable.'

'In what way?'

A muscle flicked in his jaw. 'You've only just been through a traumatic experience, and I am much more experienced than you.'

She frowned, still not getting it. 'You mean sexually?' She blinked. 'What are you afraid is going to happen? That if we sleep together again I'm going to want to marry you for *real*?' She thrust her hands on her hips, annoyance flaring. 'You're the one who proposed to *me*.'

'We can't let this get more complicated.'

'It can't get any more complicated than it already is.'

His arrogance felled her as she realised just what he was afraid of. He almost looked sheepish. Too late. She was furious.

'Newsflash, Massimo—I'm not going to *fall in love with you*. It's just sex. We've done it before and I can take it or leave it any time. It's not that amazing.'

There was a dangerous glint in his eye now that probably should have made her pause. She didn't.

'What are you afraid might happen? That I might get so addicted to sex with you I won't want our marriage to ever end?' She laughed. 'You're such a jerk. You do *not* need to worry that I'm going to deny you your divorce in the future!'

His expression hardened. 'So you've no concerns about us getting married now?'

'None at all,' she declared recklessly. 'Bring it on, Massimo. Marry me as soon as you can manage it!'

CHAPTER TWELVE

THERE WAS NO taking it back now. For once Carrie had too much pride. Besides, she'd pretty much known it would be inevitable that she would say yes to him. She'd do anything to remain central in Ana's life and she wanted her daughter to have the best—both parents in her life. But the satisfaction in squaring off with him, in calling him out on his ridiculously egotistical concerns... She'd show him.

'Here are my rules,' she said determinedly. 'We marry. But only in name. We *won't* sleep together. When we finally get the permanent leave to remain, we separate.' It was going to take years but surely she could handle it if they were physically distant within their household? 'Eventually we share custody. I'll stay in whatever city you want.'

'But for now we live together,' he insisted. 'We're *married*.'

'Defined how we want, as you first suggested. Until my residency is through.'

His jaw clenched but he nodded slowly. 'Done.'

She glared at him. She wasn't finished yet. 'Don't lie to me. Don't cheat on me. Don't make promises you can't fulfil.'

'We really don't know each other, do we?' He looked as angry as she felt.

'I guess we can be good at maintaining some distance even on tiny islands.'

'If we're going to successfully maintain a *marriage* for a few years, then we'd better change that.' He huffed a harsh breath and put his hands on his hips. 'Got any burning questions for me?'

For a split second she was shockingly distracted by his chest—her body still rebelling at the plan for them not to sleep together.

'Or do you want to start?' he asked when she remained speechless. 'So who lied? Or cheated? Or made promises they couldn't keep? What are the reasons for that specific list?'

Emotion exhausted her. From the heights of ecstasy, to brutal disappointment, to fiery rage— she'd run through it all in the last ten minutes alone. So she was in no place to hold back now. 'My fiancé nailed all three.'

'*Fiancé?*' He gaped.

'Why do you think I didn't want to marry?

There's a little more to the story of my unstoppably successful sisters.' She gritted her teeth. 'My *ex*-fiancé is now married to Maddie. My older sister.'

'Your fiancé married your *sister*?' Massimo's features sharpened. 'How is...? How did...? *What* fiancé?'

Carrie stomped to the side of the path and sat in the shade. If they were to survive a few years of a fake marriage for visa purposes, they were going to need to be civil, and he'd have to know something of her sad love life.

'I met Gabe at university. I was working on reception at the gym part-time and he came in regularly,' she explained briefly. 'He was charming, and we got talking, and I was a fool and fell for him. He studied law and I wanted to help him, you know? I like to help. I'm good at it. So I introduced him to my father and Dad offered him a summer placement.'

'At the family firm?'

She nodded. 'Gabe didn't have accommodation in the city so my parents invited him to stay with us.'

Massimo looked confused. 'Move in with you?'

'I wasn't there,' she said. 'I was working a couple of jobs on the coast for the summer. I was saving. I wanted to pay for my dress then I could pick it myself, you know?' She shook her head with a little laugh. 'Anyway, while I was away working to save for the wedding of my dreams, Gabe and Maddie couldn't help themselves.'

He took a moment. 'That must have hurt.'

She nodded slowly. 'It *sucked*.'

His frown deepened. 'You hadn't slept with him.'

She rolled her eyes. Honestly, was sex all that mattered? 'He wanted to wait til we were married. But I guess he didn't feel the same about Maddie. They were having an affair for weeks before they told me. They even consulted my family on *how* to tell me. So everyone knew for ages before I did. Everyone supported them. It was…'

'Horrible,' Massimo muttered. 'They betrayed you.'

'I love supporting them. But I would've loved *their* support too,' she said. 'Why didn't they have my back?'

'They should have,' he said. 'He was a fool, Carrie.'

She shook her head. 'No, he just wanted the prettier, smarter, skinner, sportier one.' She grimaced at her own self-pity. 'I wasn't enough for him.'

'He said that?'

She nodded slowly. 'He realised I wasn't ambitious enough for him. Or exciting enough. He'd got bored.'

Massimo was very still. 'Did you go to the wedding?'

'I did a reading.'

Massimo's thunderstruck expression actually made her giggle.

'I wasn't a bridesmaid,' she explained. 'Only my younger sister, Rosie, was. Maddie figured I wouldn't want to wear a dress with spaghetti straps because she knows I wouldn't want to show my upper arms.'

'You're showing your upper arms now. They're very nice upper arms.'

'Thank you. I don't think they're that awful either, but I guess she did.' Carrie shrugged. 'I wore a jacket and read about love and loyalty and smiled as if it didn't hurt at all.'

'And your parents let all that happen?'

'Didn't I want them to be happy?' She echoed their words. 'They thought I shouldn't mind too much because it was obvious to everyone that Gabe felt more brotherly towards me anyway.'

'Carrie—'

'It wasn't completely untrue.' She'd realised it now. 'There wasn't that spark I felt with…' Suddenly awkward, she glanced at him.

'You didn't want to make a scene in the church? Go all-out drama?'

She grinned ruefully. 'What would've been the point?'

'It might've been cathartic.'

She shook her head.

'So you said nothing and ran away.'

'Chose to travel the world, actually,' she corrected with a tilt of her chin. 'Spent all my dress money on the air ticket.'

'Far better investment.' However, he didn't smile. 'You never told them how much they'd all hurt you? Not even your parents?'

'Sometimes it's better to walk away, don't you think? There's no point fighting for something you can't ever win.'

'Doesn't mean you let them off with bad behaviour. You've called me out on it. Why not them?'

Don't interrupt my focus… Don't interrupt their training…

She'd always felt as if her concerns weren't important enough to interrupt any of them. But Massimo had wanted her to talk and he'd paid attention when she had. And he'd challenged her. He also took her seriously. And that first night he'd *wanted* distraction—he'd welcomed it as much as she had. They'd had *fun* together.

'When *are* you going to tell them about Ana?' he asked.

She sighed. 'I don't want to. I don't want their pity. *"Poor Carrie. Did you hear she had a fling and got herself knocked up and now she's a single mother and no one will ever want her now?"'*

'Is that what you think—?'

'No. I don't think that,' she interrupted him. 'I don't have *any* regrets. But that I didn't realise I was pregnant? It just adds to a long list of humiliating failures that I'm never going to live down. I just…' She shrugged. 'I've never excelled in anything the way they have.'

'Maybe you're good at different things.'

'It all depends on what's valued, right?'

'*Ana* is valued,' he pointed out. 'You ensure that. So you should tell them about her. And you should let them know they hurt you. Don't make it easy for them to get away with it. Stand up and say how you feel. Say what you want.'

He made it sound easy. And with him it had been. But with her family?

'It wouldn't make any difference,' she said.

Massimo glanced towards the sea then back at her. 'So Gabe is why you didn't want to say yes to marriage sooner?'

She braced. 'I thought he loved me and that I loved him. I was wrong on both counts. But I don't want to be hurt or humiliated like that ever again.' She swallowed. 'But this is different, right? This isn't like that at all.'

He slowly nodded. 'I won't make promises I won't keep. I won't lie. And I certainly won't cheat—I wouldn't do that to you. Or Ana. When we separate, I don't want it to hurt her.' His tone held more than a ring of authenticity. It had pain.

She knew his mother had died but had someone else betrayed him?

'Nor do I,' she said. 'She comes first, Massimo. Always. Okay?'

He gazed into her eyes for a long moment. 'That's important to you, isn't it?'

'It's everything.'

'I'll organise the wedding right away. It won't take much to arrange.'

'Right away?' She paused. 'Do you want us to get married *here*?'

'You did just challenge me to *bring it on*.' He suddenly grinned. 'So, yeah, here. As soon as possible. Are you going to argue with me?'

She *could* list a bunch of reasons why it wasn't a good idea. Except none of the objections popping in her head were insurmountable, and some rear-guard reaction to delay the inevitable was pointless. She'd said yes. She'd said what she wanted. For Ana. So she'd face it.

'Sunrise or sunset?' she asked.

Surprise lit his eyes and he leaned in. 'Which would you prefer?

'Ana will be in a good mood at sunrise,' she said pragmatically. 'One of us will be pacing with her at sunset when she's tired and grizzly. It will be easier to get through it without interruptions from her in the morning.'

'Sunrise it is.'

His easy practicality quelled her flaring nerves. They weren't going to have a wedding night. She'd ruled out sex after his arrogant declaration she was 'too vulnerable' for him to sleep with her. If they married early in the morning, it would turn into another simple day spent caring for Ana. Nothing special. This would be a passionless arrangement. She could deal with that. For sure.

We won't sleep together.

Massimo needed space and time away from

her to think. Learning about her ex and her sister only confirmed what he'd known the night they'd met—she wasn't his type. Carrie needed and wanted someone to love. She was emotionally generous—kind and caring, with an enthusiastic effervescence, and she was eternally supportive, even to her own detriment. She'd put her own study on hold to support the sister who'd then gone on to betray her. She'd worked hard for Sereana even when she'd been so sick.

And she wanted Ana to be put *first*.

She was a fighter for others. But she didn't often ask for what *she* wanted. Maybe she'd learned not to, if her family had been so busy pushing their own achievements and not recognising hers because they hadn't involved certificates or medals.

Except she'd asked for all kinds of things from *him*. That night. Just now by the rock pool. He couldn't believe he'd pulled away. He didn't know where he'd found the strength. But, agonising as it had been at the time, it was the right thing to do.

We won't sleep together.

That was good. He could never, ever give her all she really needed. Though she'd been insulted, he'd been right—she *was* too vulnerable to handle his limitations. While he could do sex without emotional involvement, he didn't think she could, and it wasn't because of her inexperience. It was because she poured all her emotion into *everything* she did. She had *integrity*. And to him that was priceless.

But he also knew that ultimately they'd want different things. Ultimately she *should* meet someone who could give her everything.

His stomach churned. She didn't like to let people down and he wouldn't let her down. He knew she worked hard because she thought she had to *earn* value. Because some jerk had told her she was boring. She was feisty and she was funny, and Massimo was filled with a horrifically Neanderthal pleasure in knowing that the jerk had never discovered just how *not* boring Carrie was. And not just in bed.

She deserved far more than he could ever offer. But she was stuck with him for the immediate future. He wished he could make it better.

The wedding of my dreams.

This was hardly going to be that. But maybe he could somehow make it a little special. He could make the effort for her—give her something of what she put in for other people.

* * *

Carrie shouldn't have been surprised to discover Massimo had their whole wedding planned only two hours after she'd accepted his proposal in a pique.

Just after lunch the next day—at the exact time on the schedule that he'd outlined to her the night before—she heard the helicopter coming in to land. But it wasn't only the lawyer and the celebrant she'd expected who were on board. Another man emerged, carrying a bunch of camera equipment. And then Sereana appeared, burdened by several garment bags.

Carrie's heart soared and she pressed her hand on Massimo's arm. 'You invited Sereana?'

That hadn't been on the schedule.

'You need an attendant.' His gaze was very warm, very green. 'Who better than Ana's namesake?'

Carrie beamed. 'Thank you.'

Massimo pressed his lips together in a tight smile and quickly strode ahead to greet the others.

After a bubbling few moments showing Sereana her villa, Carrie met Massimo and the lawyer, Jai. If the lawyer thought it odd that they were so carefully preparing for their separation, he didn't give it away. There was a sheaf of paperwork to be filled in—including Carrie's consent for a DNA test from Ana.

'It's only to ensure the visa application is as strong as possible,' Massimo said.

'I know.'

'Are you sure you don't want further independent advice?' Massimo frowned at her across the table.

'I trust you,' Carrie muttered.

Something flickered in his eyes and his mouth twitched. 'So soon?'

'I know you wouldn't want to harm Ana in any way. So you won't harm me.' But she bit her lip as she pointed to one line in the lengthy contract. 'That is too much.'

His hot, intense gaze held hers for two seconds too long. 'That settlement is barely enough to ensure Ana has the best when she is with you. You need to be safe and secure so that she is.'

It was all about Ana. All for Ana. And that was everything she wanted. Except that chemistry wouldn't wash away.

As soon as she'd signed the documents, she walked back to Sereana's villa, avidly curious about those garment bags. Her friend was stretched out on a lounger, a vibrant cocktail in hand and a broad smile on her face. 'I've met the marvellous Naomi already. She's going to do my hair. I'm in heaven, right? Because she's an angel.'

'*You're* the angel!' Carrie laughed. 'Tell me what was in all your bags!'

Were her stupidly hopeful suspicions correct?

'Only the few wedding dresses I could get in town with less than twenty-four hours' notice.' Sereana chuckled. 'Massimo said not to worry about the expense, so I didn't.'

Until Sereana had emerged with those bags, Carrie had barely thought about what she was going to wear for the ceremony at dawn tomorrow. But now it *mattered*. She wanted to look good. Frankly, suddenly she wanted to *own* this whole thing.

Sereana didn't know the truth about Carrie's relationship with Massimo, and the resort staff weren't aware it wasn't a 'real' wedding either, and, at dinner on the eve of the ceremony, everyone joined them in the large dining deck. Laughter rang out, as Massimo was in full charm mode. Seated in the centre beside him, Carrie laughed too. And, even though she knew it wasn't real, it didn't feel fraudulent. It was fun.

We won't sleep together.

She'd stipulated that and she'd be fine with it. This would be enough.

Early the next morning Sereana and Naomi, vivacious in their respective green and pink sundresses, helped Carrie get ready. Carrie knew it mightn't have the meaning of other wedding ceremonies, but this was still *her* day. Her commitment to a future for Ana, for Massimo and for herself. And, while the marriage wouldn't last, she was going to wholly commit to it now. She wasn't going to be an unwilling participant only doing it to keep the peace. She was doing it because she truly believed it was the best course of action in this circumstance. Because she'd *chosen* to. She wasn't being forced into anything— not by him, or by fate.

'He's going to die when he sees you,' Sereana said, deftly sewing in a last tuck on the feathery light dress that Carrie had chosen from the four her friend had brought with her.

'Thank you for the confidence boost.'

'You don't need it,' Sereana said.

Carrie looked in the mirror and barely recognised herself. Sereana was right. Carrie was in her dream destination, in a dress more beautiful than she could ever have imagined, with the most beautiful baby on earth, about to marry the most fascinating man on earth. *He'd be her friend going forward, right?*

She wasn't a prisoner, but a woman who wanted everything she'd signed up for.

CHAPTER THIRTEEN

MASSIMO HAD NEVER been lost for words. His ability to smooth awkward social moments had always been effortless. Now it wasn't just that he couldn't think what to say, he'd lost the physical ability to create sound at all. His throat was clogged, his mouth parched, and his tight lungs rendered breathing impossible. He felt hot, tense and uncomfortably helpless—he wasn't coping. He'd never failed to cope with anything. But watching Carrie walk down the fine sand to where he stood right by the shore was killing him.

Her long silk slip was covered by a loose gossamer-light layer of lace, creamy and hinting at such softness. She was luminous—demure yet devastatingly sensual. He couldn't stop staring, even as doing so destroyed him. Her blue eyes were as clear as the water beside them, while her hair gleamed like a rose-gold crown, and suddenly his made-to-measure linen shirt felt too small. Tongue-tied and breaking into a sweat, he was unable to tear his gaze away. And he was suddenly afraid. The temptation to take her hand—to stop her from disappearing, to keep her ethereal beauty beside him—was crippling. As for the ache to kiss her...

Why had he agreed that they wouldn't sleep together? What had he been *thinking*? He hadn't, of course. He'd been hot-headed, wanting to win, because she somehow pushed all his buttons and made him want to fight.

But as the sun sent streaks of light across the sky, and petite waves lapped at the shore, he didn't want to fight any more. He'd just drown in her eyes. He had before. Sinkingly, he knew he would again. The clogged sensation in his throat descended to his chest where his ribs weren't strong enough to contain his pounding heart.

They were only doing this for Ana. So surely he could control the physical attraction to Carrie? But all thoughts of parenting arrangements and future plans for a separate lifestyle fled from his head as she drew nearer. All he wanted was the oblivion he knew he'd find in her arms. He shouldn't have resisted the other day. Why had he thought he *could*? He didn't want to restrain anything any more. Had that rash decision not to act made their chemistry stronger than ever?

The maxim said you always wanted what you couldn't have. Maybe it was that simple and that easily resolved. If he took her back to bed, it would ease, right?

But the sexual tension tearing him apart was augmented by a sense of foreboding. He knew their marriage should make scant difference to anything. It was only to obtain a simple piece of paper for a practical purpose. It was not anything portentous. Yet he could scarcely breathe through the intensity of the damned ceremony. And why had it got to him so much when, beside him, Carrie seemed a picture of unbothered serenity? Couldn't she feel the desire screaming from his cramping muscles?

Yeah. He wanted her more than was rational or healthy. So he forced his glance away.

He saw Sereana, and Jai his lawyer, saw Ana sleeping in the nanny's arms. He saw them all. Then he chose to ignore their knowing smiles.

Carrie had to listen hard to hear over the drumming in her ears, had to breathe deeply to echo the vows that felt more permanent and more meaningful than she'd expected, had to blink and look away from the stunning decorations they'd surprised her with.

And, while she tried so hard not to stare at

Massimo, it was impossible not to. That white linen shirt made his skin all the more bronzed and in turn highlighted his eyes. He enthralled her. The barely leashed energy emanating from him was incredibly intense but she couldn't trust her ability to decode the emotional source. Was it anger or something else entirely? She wanted to be alone with him so she could ask. So she could… *No. There'll be none of that, remember?* Thankfully the officiating went relatively quickly.

Vows? Check.

Rings?

She was thrown when Jai presented a small woven basket to them both. There weren't two but *three* rings nestling on the layer of soft fabric inside. First Massimo slid a solid gold band on her finger, then a ring with an enormous ocean-blue stone in the centre. She put the remaining ring onto his finger. He flipped his wrist to keep hold of her hand. Distracted by that enormous stone, by the pulse in her heart skipping fast and faster, she let him.

'Carrie?'

A quiet call to complete the ceremony.

Vows. Ring. *Kiss.*

It was time for the kiss. *Awkward.*

She lifted her chin. A peck would do, right?

His grip on her hand tightened. A tug pulled her closer. It wasn't a peck. Carrie's eyes closed as he gave her the gentlest reverential kiss—a promise of something richer, sweeter, more nuanced than any before. She lifted her hand to his chest, unable to restrain the rush of desire, of reciprocation. The kiss changed. Deepened. Provocative and lush, it was a gift that took at the same time.

Her fingers curled into his shirt. She wanted to shred the soft linen to feel his skin against hers. Distantly she heard cheering, a little laughter and applause. Too late, she remembered there were witnesses—an *audience*, in fact, because this was a *performance*. It hadn't served any other purpose, or meant anything more to him. And they weren't doing lust. They'd agreed on that. Yet she knew in her bones that to be false. The chemistry was undeniable and had not yet burned out.

'Do we need all these photos?' she asked quietly as she held Ana, posing for what felt like aeons after the ceremony.

'For immigration,' Massimo explained. 'We need everything documented and looking legitimate.'

Did that have to mean images of her all but swooning in his arms? With crushed petals at their feet, releasing an intoxicating romantic perfume and blurring her reality? With Ana gurgling in delight as Massimo teased them both into giggling?

Finally, Massimo went to the photographer, checking the images to ensure they were enough. Carrie sought out Sereana for some respite but, to her disappointment, her friend had already changed and was now waiting by the helicopter pad.

'Are you not staying longer?' Carrie asked. 'Not even for breakfast?'

'You newlyweds need to be alone.' Sereana's infectious laugh rang across the grounds. 'I'll come back another time. Massimo has offered the resort for my family and I whenever we want.'

It wasn't only Sereana who left. The lawyer, officiant and photographer all went with her. And, then to Carrie's surprise, relief descended. The show was over. Ana's future was secure. It was all going to be okay, right?

'Leah still has Ana, so you can get changed if you'd like.' Massimo watched her approach the dining table, where he was drinking coffee.

'Do I need to?' She rather loved her dress. She

liked the way it swished around her legs and the lace overlay felt cool. 'I could wear this all day.'

'Sure, stay in it,' he said tightly. 'You're remarkably relaxed.'

'What I am,' she suddenly realised, 'Is ravenous.'

She'd been too busy to eat breakfast before but, now the vows were done, she needed...a displacement activity. Something to stop her looking to where he sat in the shade, watching her.

'Are you?' His voice sounded oddly tight again.

'Yeah.' She selected a croissant, tearing the fresh, warm folds of golden pastry with her fingers. 'It's good that's done. I don't know why I was worried. It's going to be fine.'

Massimo refilled his coffee cup, only almost to empty it in one gulp. How he could drink it scalding hot like that? Maybe he wasn't as easy about their marriage as he made out but, with their pre-marital agreement already signed, it wouldn't be for ever. *That* thought vanquished both her hunger and her relief. She abandoned the rest of the croissant.

'Are you satisfied already?' he asked.

There was a dangerous edge to his question that made her feel a sudden need to escape.

'Where's Leah?' She glanced around. 'I can take Ana now.'

'I think Leah planned to settle her for a nap.'

'Oh.' Carrie's pulse skittered. 'Then I might paddle before it gets too hot.'

After that she'd get out of her dress and the day would carry on as if it were like any other they'd had here. Resting. Reading. Dipping in the water. Cradling Ana.

Without waiting for Massimo's reply, she walked down to the water. She'd avoid her feelings for him. Avoid *him* altogether. It was too huge for her to handle. How could she ever comprehend the absurdly shocking fact that the man was her *husband*?

'Carrie.'

He'd followed her.

She turned. The look in his eyes reset her again. Electricity crackled, drowning her recently resurrected anxiety. And, of all the volatile, mercurial emotions he inspired in her, desire was the most constant.

'Are you running away?' he asked.

'Not a strong enough swimmer, sadly.' She waved at the islands in the distance. 'So I'm resigned to my fate.'

'What fate do you think that is?' He gave a half-smile as he stepped closer.

His tease reminded her of how he'd been the night they'd met. Charming and playful. Yet there was that tension underlying their spark. Neither of them could escape. Not then. And they were bound together differently now. This couldn't be like that reckless, carefree night. Desperate for distraction, she stared at the rings adorning her finger. The stunning solitaire gleamed more brilliantly than the mid-morning sun.

'It's a blue diamond,' he muttered. 'If it's not the right size, we can get it altered when we get to Sydney.'

It fit her perfectly. As had the clothes. From only that one night, he'd gathered all kinds of information about her. Maybe he could accurately guess a woman's size from one glance. The thought didn't make her feel great.

'Did you get it in Suva?' she asked.

'No, I brought all the rings with me.'

She was shocked enough to draw a breath but at the same time wasn't surprised. 'You were that sure I would say yes?'

'I made the plan.'

And she'd fallen into step with it.

'Do your plans ever fail?'

'All the time. I just adapt.'

She didn't believe him. He worked to ensure he won. Always. A wave of melancholy washed through her. 'How are you going to outdo this next time?' she asked. 'When you get married for real?'

'*We're* married for real,' he said quietly. 'I have no plans to marry a second time.'

'But our marriage *will* end.'

He shrugged. 'Then I'll go back to being single.'

'So you can play the field?'

'Is that so awful?'

'You don't ever want to settle down?'

He shook his head. 'Now I have an heir to inherit all the things. This whole situation is surprisingly convenient.'

'You think?'

He stared at her, the facade of teasing humour dropped. 'No. It's frustrating as hell.'

She stood still. 'What do you want to do about that?'

'What do I want to do?' he echoed in a furious whisper. 'I want to peel that dress off you. Very slowly. Very carefully. And then—' He broke off to drag in a ragged breath. 'I am so sick of fighting it. I am so sick of trying not to…'

'Not to what?'

'Touch you.'

The desire neither of them wanted yet neither could resist took control.

'Then *why* insist on trying?'

Emotion flared in his eyes. 'Because we're not sleeping together.' But he held out his hand.

And, with a boldness she'd felt only around him, Carrie took it and tugged *him* closer to her. 'Who said anything about sleeping?'

Carrie lost herself in the kiss. The drive to dive into his arms was irresistible. She'd never imagined that, the next time she touched him like this, she would be his *wife*.

It doesn't mean anything. It's just for immigration purposes. It's pure practicality.

But he shot her a look of such hot possessiveness that she nearly crisped to a cinder on the spot. He made her feel wanted in a way no one had ever made her feel wanted. But it was a falsity, wasn't it? Because it was Ana he wanted. Security for their baby. Not really her. But in this moment Ana wasn't here. She was safe with Leah. And Massimo had followed Carrie down to the water. Now they faced each other on the edge of the world. Alone. And what she wanted was reflected in his eyes. In this instant there was only them and, on this one, most basic of levels, they were equal in terms of desire. So she let him sweep her off her feet. She let him carry her up to the privacy of his spacious villa. She would let him do everything this moment. And he knew it.

But, as he peeled the filmy fabric from her skin, the glide of his hands over her body was too gentle.

'You're recovering well,' he muttered. That tightness, that ragged jerk of his breath, told her so much.

'Yes.' She was healthy and strong and he didn't need to worry. She was only going to break if he *didn't* give her the release she'd been craving so long. She reached for him with hungry hands. 'Massimo.'

He shook his head, shuddering as she touched him. He lifted her on to his big bed.

'I want everything. Fast, slow, now!' He half-laughed, half-choked. 'There are no half-measures for me. Not with you.'

'Good.' Because that was what she wanted too. 'So hurry up.'

His kiss was catastrophic for her control. Her response the same for his. Together they toppled into a fast, furious, panting, desperate need for completion.

'It's been so long.' He growled as he braced above her.

But at those words she turned her face away. How long was 'so long' for him? She didn't want to think of him with anyone else. Certainly not right now. But he gently turned her face back round and his green eyes saw right through her.

'There hasn't been anyone since you,' he muttered fiercely as he reclaimed possession of her. 'Not in months and months and months.' His mutter became a growl. 'And I am not going to last as long as I'd like because you're so hot. So soft.'

Shaking, she sighed in pure pleasure. The vulnerability in this was too exquisite, too precious, not to share and reciprocate. 'There hasn't been anyone *but* you.'

He closed his eyes. 'I'm glad. I know that makes me…'

'Human.'

She was human too. She was unbearably glad there'd been no one else for him. At the very least, they had this, and this was magic. He weaved his fingers through her hair to tilt her face towards his.

'More.' He demanded. He devoured. 'More.'

CHAPTER FOURTEEN

MASSIMO RECLINED ON the sun lounger, holding his sleeping daughter in his arms as he surveyed the scene from behind the safety of his aviators. He'd never considered the meditative powers of a sleeping infant before, but he'd never remained so still for so long in his life. Usually he was a perpetual-motion machine, moving from one thing to the next, to the next, and the next. Holding tiny Ana, he couldn't do that. It had led to a lax attitude to his work—he'd barely thought about it.

Rather, it was Carrie who fascinated him. He couldn't stop staring as she languorously stretched out in the pool. Maybe she'd been right to accuse him of arrogance in assuming that she'd want more from him emotionally if they slept together again. Maybe he'd been wrong after all. She'd adamantly insisted she wasn't going to fall for him, and right now she seemed as happy as him to keep conversation light and the nights very, very long. She accepted that their marriage would end in the medium term. But a stray thought lifted as something in his gut tensed.

Maybe this arrangement could last longer than the length of time required to satisfy immigration requirements. Arranged marriages worked all the world over, so why not theirs? Essentially that was what it was—a practical union based in practical need, not the vagaries of emotion. They could provide Ana with a stable home, two parents who were there for her—the things he wanted his gorgeous baby to have. The things he hadn't had.

Carrie had been engaged once before. She'd cared enough about another man to say yes to him and she'd not wanted to do that again. Massimo had assured her this was different. It was because it was an *arrangement*. They could keep it this easy. Not emotionally intense. Not destructive. They could keep it safe for all of them. But a twinge of discomfort pulled between his shoulder blades.

'Why the frown?' Carrie called softly from the water.

'Ana's stirring.' He swung his legs down and stood. He waded in to let Ana feel the water, staying at the shaded end of the pool. She gurgled as he gently sprinkled her.

'She's a mermaid.' Carrie swam closer.

'Like her mother.'

Truthfully Carrie was more of a siren, summoning him to his sensual destruction. And he couldn't get enough of it. He figured it would settle down when they returned to Australia. He'd be busy back at work and she'd have her own projects. She'd already promised to keep supporting Sereana remotely. But life *would* be different for her. His wealth engendered a certain public interest and she was going to have to navigate that. It would be intense—at least initially. He just knew she wasn't going to be keen. The tension in his shoulders tightened more.

He didn't want to go back to Sydney yet. He wanted to play in the water and share knowing smiles with Carrie as they cared for Ana. They were a *unit* and he'd never been part of such a thing before. He wanted to savour it. And, as much as he wanted to take Carrie to bed this second, he wasn't going to summon Leah to mind Ana. He was going to wait. Not even when Carrie climbed out of the pool and lay on the lounger, and he had to gaze at her beautiful curves, did he give in to the temptation. She needed rest.

'I've never been anywhere as beautiful as this.'

Her drowsy gaze tracked him as he paced slowly around the pool, keeping Ana content.

Wanting Carrie while not wanting this precious moment with both her and Ana to end was the sweetest torture. So in the hour that he cradled the baby and watched Carrie sleep he planned exactly what he was going to do once he was finally alone with her tonight.

That evening he uncovered the hot tub on his private deck, feeling Carrie's full attention on him as he worked. The low flame from a brazier illuminated her face, casting her in a golden glow. Her hair was swept up into a messy knot while the rings he'd given her sparkled intermittently as they caught the light.

'Is it ready?' Her husky voice betrayed her need.

He'd already seen the smoke in her eyes and felt the electricity all though the dinner he'd deliberately lingered over. But that tension tightened. He needed to prepare her properly. And she needed to prepare her family.

'My assistant is going to send a media release out before we leave Fiji,' he said as she stepped into the heated water. 'There'll be attention when we land in Sydney. You might want to inform your family. They'll get some calls.'

'Media calls?' Her startled expression turned comical. 'But my family live on the other side of the world.'

'I have business interests all over the world, and this isn't expected from me. They're going to make a meal of it.'

He sat across from her in the water and watched as the smoke in her eyes evaporated.

'So I have to...'

'You're going to have to tell them at some point,' he reasoned. 'You have a child. You're *married.*' Protectiveness rose inside as reluctance blanched her face. 'You're afraid of their reaction?'

'I know I shouldn't let it get to me. I know it's not rational.'

'They're your family. Rational doesn't factor into it. And when you've been hurt...' He shrugged.

She looked at him steadily. 'I guess I could phone them now,' she said valiantly. 'The time difference works. And I'm relaxed. I couldn't be anywhere more beautiful...'

Honestly, the last thing he wanted this second was for her to phone her parents, but it was also something she *needed* to get done.

'It's perfect timing,' he lied.

She laughed. 'No, it isn't.'

'There's never going to be a perfect time,' he pointed out.

She stared at him for a long moment, then snatched up his phone from the deck. He unlocked it and then she tapped in the number.

'Carolyn!' Her mother's voice carried clear in the still night the second Carrie had greeted her. 'Oh, it's such good timing that you've called. Maddie is here with Gabe. They've got marvellous news.'

Massimo narrowed his eyes—would that be the betraying sister and ex?

'Have they? That sounds exciting.' Carrie managed a smile.

It turned out Maddie had a new job *and* she and Gabe were expecting. Massimo winced at her mother's utter lack of sensitivity, but Carrie kept the smile and congratulated them. Minutes passed as Carrie listened to more detail, more drama, before her mother seamlessly moved on to a description of her other sister's last event and then segued into an update of her latest case.

To Massimo's increasing displeasure, she hadn't even asked Carrie how she was, let alone given her any chance to share her *own* news. Her mother didn't seem able to *listen*. Massimo raised his brows meaningfully.

Her gaze still locked on him, Carrie took a breath.

'Look, I'm sorry to interrupt, but I really do need to tell you a couple of things.' She finally cut off her mother's endless update. 'I've met someone. I met him a while back, actually.'

'Oh, that's nice,' her mother said glibly. 'That reminds me, I forgot to tell you about—'

'Mum, I got married,' Carried interrupted bluntly.

'What?'

'Here. In Fiji. I got married.'

Finally, there was a pause. Albeit brief. 'But you wanted to get married in Isherwood Hall.'

Carrie's jaw dropped. 'That's where Maddie and Gabe got married.'

Her older sister and her ex again... Massimo frowned. Why hadn't this woman asked her daughter just *who* it was she'd married? Why wasn't she interested in what was *important*— her own daughter's happiness?

'Exactly,' her mother gushed. 'It was beautiful. You've wanted to get married there since you were a little girl.'

The wedding of her dreams? Massimo moved

through the water to put his hands on Carrie's shoulders. Her eyes were heartachingly shiny but she sent him a half-smile. 'Well, I had a lovely ceremony on the beach at dawn. It was very special. And there's more.' She drew another breath. 'I had a baby a few weeks ago.'

'What?' Her mother's voice leapt an octave. 'Don't be silly. We saw that picture of you just recently.'

Carrie frowned. 'What picture?'

'With the athletes at that meet in Fiji. Did you run the race or were you just on the admin side again?'

Were you just...again...?

Massimo clenched his jaw to stop himself saying something unforgivable. But he felt Carrie straighten beneath his hands.

'My daughter's name is Ana,' she said, suddenly calm, suddenly strong, as she looked at him. 'My husband's name is Massimo Donati-Wells. He's quite well-known over here. You might get some people asking about it.'

'Massimo Dona-*what*? Never heard of him.'

Amusement flashed in her eyes then. With a grin, Massimo leaned closer and rested his forehead against hers. To his delight she leaned back, her blue gaze still locked on his. He liked the connection. He didn't want her to be alone in this. She needed a sideline supporter.

'I just wanted to let you know before you found out from someone else,' she said. 'I have to go now. It's very late over here. I'll send photos in the morning.'

'But, Carrie...' Her mother sounded confused. 'Are you sure you don't want to talk to Maddie?'

'No, I really need to go.'

There was a silence after she ended the call.

'I'm sorry, Carrie,' he said.

'I always hope it might be different. But it never is. They're just...'

'Self-centred?' He shook his head in amazement. 'But what was the photo she meant?'

'I've no idea. Something on social media? My sisters are all over it.'

He took the phone from her and did a quick social media search.

'Oh.' Carrie stared as he turned the phone so they could both see the result. 'I didn't know Sereana had posted that. Or that my family would have been interested in seeing it.'

No wonder her mother had laughed at the idea she'd had a baby. In the photo, a group of athletes stood smiling at the camera. Carrie was on the far left of the line-up next to Sereana. Her silky hair was shining and she looked carefree and happy.

Massimo's throat thickened. Her radiant face looked only a little softer about the edges and her sundress hung simply. She didn't look pregnant at all—certainly not as if she was about to give birth. But she had—just *three days* after this photo was taken.

'Where *did* you hide her?' His words sounded raspy.

'I've no idea. I thought the backaches were tweaks from sleeping in a different bed.' She smiled sheepishly. 'My waist was a bit thicker. Like, my jeans were a struggle to do up. But I thought that was just a few extra comfort-eating kilos. It wasn't all centred in a lump out front, you know?'

It sure hadn't been. His skin prickled. Comfort-eating because she'd *needed* comfort. Because she'd been sad and alone. Because he'd been a jerk when she'd called him.

'I'm sorry I didn't believe you when you first told me,' he said huskily.

Not only had her family not listened to her, neither had he.

'I don't blame you,' she said stoically. 'It's pretty unusual.'

But he hated thinking how alone she'd been. He knew she'd not spoken up more because she'd never had *anyone* really listen to her. Her family were too busy and clearly didn't value what she had to offer. While he'd shut her down because he'd been *unable* to listen because of his own fears. So she'd had to deal with everything alone.

How he'd treated her haunted him. It wasn't her fault—his reaction hadn't really been *anything* to do with her. It hadn't been because he'd not valued her in that way. He wanted her to know that.

'*You'd* done nothing to make me mistrustful,' he muttered. 'I was that way long before I met you.'

He didn't trust anyone. He hadn't for a long time. People died or lied or left. Always.

She stilled. 'Why?'

He couldn't look away from the gentle question in her eyes. She was alone too, yet she still reached out, offering support. She knew he hurt and she wanted to help. But that wasn't why he wanted to tell her. He wanted to *explain* his own shoddy behaviour to her. Not to excuse it, but so she could understand it hadn't been about her.

'I always believed Mum was the love of my father's life,' he said gruffly, turning to sit beside her in the warm water. 'She was *everything* to him, and when she died he effectively died too. Emotionally. He was so lost in grief he couldn't really function, and certainly couldn't look at me.'

'Your eyes?' she muttered softly.

He grimaced. 'My nanny tried to tell me it wasn't *me*. It was that he loved my mother so much that he couldn't cope with her loss.'

'Massimo…'

He didn't want to feel love like that. To be so enthralled by someone that life was destroyed when that person left.

'But it *was* me. He hadn't wanted me. He'd wanted her. *Only* her. When I was a kid he told me he'd only agreed to try for a baby because it was what *she'd* wanted, and that he'd hated how unhappy she was every month when she found she wasn't pregnant. That all those years of trying ruined their happy marriage.'

'He actually *said* that to you?'

'Because it was my fault she was dead. Only a couple of hours after I was born, she had a massive stroke and died.'

He had only one photo of her holding him, when he was only minutes old. It was his most treasured possession. His father had destroyed the rest in a rage just over a decade later. It was why he'd wanted all those photos from their wedding day for Ana. Massimo wanted her to know her mother adored her. And her father.

'She'd been his world and she was gone, and that was because of me. So I had a nanny until I was sent to boarding school. Dad hadn't wanted to retain the nanny for my holidays, so then there was a succession of them. A temporary carer for each break. Some interested. Most not.'

'There was no stability for you,' she said. 'No one you could trust.'

He sighed heavily. 'Anyway, I used to get sore throats as a kid, and eventually I needed an operation. As part of the pre-op procedures, they tested my blood type. Dad said it wasn't necessary because both he and my mother were quite a rare blood type. The *same* blood type.'

'Massimo...'

'Yeah. Turns out I'm a blood type that's impossible for my parents to have produced together. Which means my father...'

She drew in a steadying breath. 'Is not your biological father.'

'My mother lied to get pregnant,' he mumbled. 'She had an affair.'

He had to look away from Carrie. The look in her eyes was troubled and too tender and he wanted to tumble into her in *every* way. Not this time. He gazed up at the stars instead. There were so many, they reminded him he was a mere speck.

'I found him through a DNA search,' he finally said. 'Apparently they were acquaintances. The guy admitted he'd always wanted her but he didn't want *me*. I was never meant to have found out.'

'And your father—when he found out?'

'I was thirteen when he walked out of that hospital and didn't come back.'

'What?' The water splashed as she twisted to face him fully. 'When you were having that operation?'

Alone and unwanted, the world he knew in ruins... Everything he'd believed in had been destroyed—his father's rejection of his mother. That such an intense love could be rejected so completely had stunned him. After that, nothing could have been certain or safe.

'It was hard enough when I reminded her of what he'd lost, but when I became proof that the woman he'd loved had actually betrayed him...'

'Massimo...'

He tried to smile but he couldn't. 'Her death had devastated him, but discovering that? He'd rejected her completely. And, by extension, me—completely. I wasn't his son. He wanted nothing more to do with me.' Massimo hadn't been able to trust anything or anyone after that. 'He sent me to several different boarding schools overseas after that. A new one each year, ostensibly to learn more languages and get the very best education.'

'That was so much change for you.' She frowned. 'Constant change.'

'I actually thought if I could become successful he might be interested in seeing me again. Stupid, huh? That I could prove myself worthy enough to be back in his life.'

His father had been a partner in a multi-national finance firm. Massimo had gone out alone. Taking on higher risk because he had nothing to lose.

'I thought that if I succeeded in his area he'd realise he'd had some influence on me...that I *was* his son in a way.'

Her expression melted. 'But that didn't happen?'

'The only positive he acknowledged was that my business success enabled him to stop supporting me financially.' He sighed.

He'd never been enough to cause his father to push beyond that anger.

'I'm so sorry, Massimo,' Carrie said quietly.

'My mother ruined her marriage to get me. Then I took her life from her.' His whole being was a destructive force. 'If I hadn't been conceived, if I hadn't been born, then she'd still be alive and they would still be happy.'

'It was a terrible *tragedy* that took her,' Carrie said. 'And it was terrible that he took it out on you.'

'He loved too hard. And he was hurt,' Massimo replied tautly.

'But that didn't mean he had to hurt you. *None* of this was your fault. He should have been there for you. He should have loved you for who you are. Just *you*.' She frowned. 'And, if he loved her so much, why couldn't he find a way to forgive her? She must have felt so desperate.'

'Which is why it's foolish to love, right?' Massimo said stiffly. 'People sacrifice too much to accommodate someone else. They compromise. Then it turns to resentment and regret, and inevitably someone lies. Someone leaves.'

'*Not* inevitably. People make it work all the time. Maybe they just communicate more,' Carrie argued. 'They discuss their dreams, take turns and grow in the same path so there's no resentment. Only reward.'

He couldn't help a small smile. 'Ever the optimist.'

Despite the heartbreak her own family caused her. But what she'd described was what she wanted—the kind of thing he couldn't do.

She swallowed. 'Will you tell him about Ana?'

The fierce need to protect Ana locked his muscles. 'You think I should?'

'Not necessarily.' A sad expression flickered across her face. 'Sometimes you need to know when to let go. When you've tried so hard…why continually put yourself up for repeated rejection? I guess it's a balance about being open to reconciliation but protecting yourself at the same time.'

Did she feel rejected repeatedly? That she was never enough?

'So that's why you're on the other side of the world—protecting yourself from your family's constant self-centredness?' he asked.

'I stay in touch but on my terms.' She nodded. 'But maybe you're right. Maybe I should have told them how it really made me feel all this time. I still didn't—not even just now.'

'You did make her shut up and listen eventually,' he said wryly.

'Only because my news was so shocking.' She

cupped his face. 'But what your father did, that's a whole other level. I'm so sorry, Massimo.'

He couldn't listen. He didn't want her pity, he wanted her body. It was the perfect antidote. He pulled her onto his lap. 'It's okay.'

'It's not.' She breathed and leaned closer. 'You're hurt.'

'So are you.' He skimmed his hands over her waist beneath the water. 'So let's feel better together. Let's forget.'

But her sweet lips twisted. 'You *can't* forget. It'll still be there.' She placed her hand over his heart. 'It's always there, whether you can bear to admit it or not.'

'Shh.' He didn't want to hear it. He only wanted the physical relief to be found with her.

She wrapped her legs around his waist and gazed into his eyes but for once he couldn't keep looking at her. She saw too much. So he buried his face into the side of her neck, breathing her scent, tasting her soft, warm skin. And somehow that was worse.

'You don't feel better by forgetting,' she whispered. 'You feel better by *sharing*.'

She was wrong. Sex was an escape. It was mindless. It was only about the release of tension and the chemical high of orgasms. The pain beating beneath her hand was something he could ignore most of the time. But now she'd mentioned it, now she touched it, she'd made it real. And now he couldn't push past it.

'Carrie.' He tensed.

'I know.' She didn't release him. Instead she embraced him more. Soft and warm and passionate. She moved with him. She wouldn't let him be alone. Be isolated. Not with her.

'Let me take it,' she muttered.

'No.' But he grabbed her thighs, holding her where he needed her. He could hardly resist— not what she was doing or offering. 'You have enough.'

'Then I'll share mine too.'

A surge of energy roared within—the hurt, the longing. It was like a crust of protection had been torn from him, revealing the ache beneath. He reached right round her to haul her closer still, needing the balm of her satiny skin and the snug heat of her welcome. More than that, he needed her strength as she coiled more tightly around him, even as he savagely drove into her.

He growled. This wasn't sex, this pulsing, raw emotion. He didn't want to frighten her with his physicality, but the depth of feeling it betrayed frightened the hell out of him. The howling ache of pain, of need, pushed him to drive harder, deeper still. But she didn't flinch. She didn't try to soothe him with words any more, only with actions, with an embrace like no other. Because there was desperation in her embrace too. In the way she clung, her legs wrapped around him, tightly accepting the raging conflict within him. Hurt transformed into action. The need to drive harder. To get closer still.

'I can take it,' she assured him huskily, and it was all he needed.

His hands tightened on her as the storm overtook him. From intimacy, to surging emotion, to a sudden need for stillness. The need to look straight into her eyes and see the safe harbour she offered. He paused on the brink—locked in stasis, of yearning so intense he thought he might die.

'Carrie.' His voice cracked.

'I'm here.'

His orgasm was as cerebral as it was physical. More emotional than anything. And he was lost.

CHAPTER FIFTEEN

How did you produce a baby that beautiful?

CARRIE ANSWERED HER mother's text message by
sending a photo of Massimo. Her mother's reply
was instant.

How did YOU meet HIM?!!!

Because it was unbelievable, right? That someone like him could have wanted someone like
her.

But he didn't want her as much now. Since that
night in the hot tub two nights ago, Massimo had
stepped back. Apparently a large deal required
urgent attention, so he was preoccupied, frowning at his screen as he worked in the shade up on
his deck for hours. She didn't disturb him and
he didn't come to her for distraction. She knew
he had massive business responsibilities, that he
had a lot of people counting on him. She could
rationalise the changes in his behaviour. But she
could also over-think and doubt everything.

It was too abrupt. Too near to that night under the stars when they'd become too close for his comfort. She knew he was a man used to being in control and it wasn't something he wanted to relinquish. That he'd come apart so completely in her arms had filled her with wonder at first, but his silence since… Didn't he trust that she'd never abuse that intimacy? But he'd suffered so much in his life—such unfair blame, such hurtful secrets exposed, such abandonment. No wonder he never trusted anyone.

On the third day of his self-imposed isolation, he came to her room. He stood on the threshold, his fists in his pockets. 'We need to go back to Sydney.'

Her heart crushed at his clipped tone but she didn't argue. She'd known that everything would change once he'd got what he'd wanted. And all he'd wanted, *really*, was Ana's security. She understood now why he'd wanted that so very much. The fantasy was over and she was going to have to figure out how to cope in his real world. It was so different from hers.

Two days later she followed him as he carried Ana through the customs facilities reserved for ultra-wealthy travellers who required ultimate privacy.

'We make a good team, Carrie,' he said. 'Our partnership is legitimate.'

But he meant in the *business* sense more than the married sense. And it wasn't true. She didn't fly in private jets. She didn't fit into this lifestyle, with sleekly groomed assistants offering to accommodate her every whim. With uniformed drivers chauffeuring them to his sophisticated Sydney apartment. She didn't know how to deal with them or his other employees or friends or ex-lovers…and she was bound to meet a few of those soon, wasn't she?

Insecurity raged. Most of all because he was so remote. The playful guy who'd stolen time for fun with her, who'd talked intimately with her, had vanished. In the real world, that guy rarely showed. And he didn't reach for her.

Massimo's Shock Marriage!
Billionaire's Baby Stunner!

The headlines in the Sydney gossip columns screamed. But it was the *baby* who was the stunner, not the bride. The conjecture was endless—when and where and how they'd met, rumours of his island retreat. The constant questions drained the last of her bleeding-out confidence.

Massimo was at work all day and at his tablet

or on more business calls all evening until she went to bed. Alone. The workaholic was in his element. That was *fine*. She'd been prepared for that. He had other priorities—of course he did. People always did. She had to get her head round Sydney, round a new routine with Ana and Leah and round ideas for her own future career. She wasn't worried. Much. Only all the time. Because he didn't hold her gaze the same. He didn't tease her.

He didn't take the *time*. For Ana, yes—an hour before he left for work, and he made the effort to be back in the evening for her bath. But other than that he'd all but disappeared into his work.

It hurt. Had their time together just been an island holiday interlude for him? Had she imagined the intense intimacy they'd shared? Doubt nibbled all belief in her decisions.

She stared at her reflection, wondering whether the dress she'd chosen was appropriate, whether she should have tied up her hair, whether she was going to be able to make polite conversation at all. They had to go to some fund-raising event— her first outing as his wife. But he'd not yet arrived home and they were supposed to have left ten minutes ago.

'You're ready?' Massimo walked in and barely glanced at her.

'Yes.'

Anger flickered in her veins at his briskness. She was *trying* but he didn't seem to be. But she couldn't summon the courage to call him out on it. Her world felt too precarious—as if there were seismic danger just beneath the surface and it would take nothing to set it off. Simply put, she was too scared she would lose *everything*.

Massimo couldn't stand to look at her. She was stunning in that sleeveless black dress, and he just wanted to walk her backwards until she was against the wall, where he'd part her legs and ravish her hard.

No. He had to retain in control. Perspective. *Distance.* He'd lost all of it that night in Fiji after she'd phoned her parents and he'd told her everything. He'd been engulfed by a firestorm of emotion that had felt insanely good.

Until the next day. He'd woken up. Completely.

He shouldn't have told her about his parents. Dredging it up, discussing it, had made him think more about it than he'd ever let himself before. And he couldn't stop comparing his parents' relationship to theirs. He didn't want Carrie to be unable to ask for what she really wanted from him, or be afraid of *hurting* him if she asked for more than he could give. Because she'd seen his hurt. And he'd never let anyone see that before. He hated that she knew he was vulnerable. And what was missing within him was never going to be fixed.

Carrie needed laughter, light and love and she *deserved* those things. But she was stuck, married to him, and he couldn't give her any of them for long—certainly not *love*. Because his family's kind of love wasn't healthy. It was desperate, controlling and destructive.

So he reshaped his plan. He pulled away because she was too true, too soft. He couldn't let her fall for him but she would. They'd have to stop sleeping together, separate sooner. He just had to get through now. Going out was the only way he could resist the ache to take her in a storm of lust this second.

Carrie tried to smile but the intimidation factor was off the scale. The other guests at the exhibition were works of art themselves. All beautiful specimens of humanity. But it wasn't just their looks. They were superstars like her sisters, like Massimo too. She paled next to them.

She'd slowly disappear and become invisible to them. to him too. But right now they all turned and stared.

'*You're* Massimo's new wife?'

Carrie wasn't quite sure how to interpret the woman's emphasis, but she determinedly smiled back. '*Only* wife, as far as I'm aware.'

'I helped him pull together your wardrobe,' the woman informed her with a speculative gleam. 'I'm Janelle. I own the department store he favours. He was very particular in what he wanted you to have. I've never known Massimo to take such an interest in dressing a woman...'

'He's usually interested only in undressing them.' The man next to Janelle made the obvious unfunny joke. 'But how lovely to have him provide you with a completely new wardrobe.'

Their words were veiled in amusement, in a light, joking tone, but the looks were sly, the speculation that he was with her only because of Ana obvious.

Of course it was obvious. They all knew he would never have married her if it hadn't been for Ana and Carrie knew that better than anyone. But suddenly she was too angry to feel inferior about it. Not tonight. Never.

'Oh, yes,' she agreed. 'I'm terribly lucky.'

'And it's most unusual for him to abandon his empire for so long.' They glanced at her sideways.

'Well, I did have his baby,' Carrie said, boldly referencing the thing they were so shocked about.

'Very clever of you, I must say.' Janelle smiled.

'Well…' Recklessly Carrie matched the woman's tone. 'I did want to bag a wealthy husband.'

'Carrie?' Massimo suddenly materialised right beside her. The man must have had ears like a bat.

'It's all right, darling.' She turned and smiled sharply. 'Your charming friend Janelle was just admiring my cleverness in conceiving your child. Naturally, I'm in complete agreement. Now, I'm going for some air.' She handed him her drink and walked out.

'What did you just say to my wife?'

Behind her Massimo was the embodiment of arctic fury. But Carrie kept walking. She made it onto the balcony. She was winded by their attack but her breath was truly stolen by her own audacity. What the hell was wrong with her? She'd just created a *scene*. She didn't do drama—not even when her sister had taken up with her fiancé with her family's full approval. But it had been impossible not to react to that remark.

A heartbeat later, Massimo joined her on the balcony, fire swirling in his eyes.

'I'm not going to apologise,' she said. In truth she was seconds away from grovelling and stammering, *Sorry!* 'I've had enough, Massimo. I'm not going to be treated like an idiot. Or underestimated. Or put up with people just being plain rude to my face.'

'Quite right.' The air crackled with energy he was barely containing. 'I completely agree, and just told them the same. Less politely.'

'You what? But they're—'

'Rude. As you said.'

She took a breath. She'd just wrecked their first social 'showing'. She wasn't the stunning, socially adept superstar wife they all expected him to have. Not the wife he *needed.* 'How did they react?'

'Don't know. Don't care. Came after you.' He stared down at her and visibly tried to steady his breathing. 'Is it okay if I come nearer?'

'Why are you asking?' she asked. 'Are you afraid I might do you harm?'

'Just want to give you the option.'

'Make me feel as if I have some control?'

'You do,' he said. 'I think you have it all, Carrie.'

To her horror, her eyes suddenly filled with

tears. Because he didn't mean that in the way she wanted him to.

'I'm sorry.' Fire still raged in his eyes. 'I didn't think they'd be so blatant.'

Of course they thought he was only with her because of the baby. It was true. The last few days had proven it—he'd had enough of anything intimate with her.

With an indecipherable mutter, Massimo pulled her into his arms and pressed his mouth to hers. And she, sad creature that she was, leaned in and took it all. Because that electricity shocked her to life. Their chemistry resulted in the kind of kiss *not* supposed to occur in public situations. The kind of kiss she'd desperately, desperately, missed and so badly needed.

But it was only moments before he tore away from her. 'We need to get out of here. Now.'

She almost stumbled as he grabbed her hand and marched her to the stairwell. 'Aren't we going to say goodbye?'

'No.'

Her pulse roared as she registered his intention. And it was totally fine by her.

They were silent in the car. Silent in the lift. Silent until they'd both stepped inside the apartment and he'd carefully closed their bedroom door so they wouldn't wake Ana or the nanny. And then…

Massimo turned to her, wildness filling his head and heart. He smashed his mouth over hers—demanding more than he ever had before, stripped right back to raw sexuality. There was no veneer of polite hesitation, of careful courtesy, and her acquiescence wasn't needed because she was the same—stripped right back to raw emotion, needing him so much she was shaking. He *had* to answer that need. He couldn't leave her trembling, alone and aching. Not his brave, honest, generous lover.

With voracious urgency he dropped to his knees, worshipping the woman he wanted more than his next breath. He was completely lost to the power of his desire, not just for her, but to please her. He peeled aside her panties. He'd make her come. Now. Hard. On his tongue. Because giving her pleasure was the one thing he could do for her. He could make her feel good. He could make her forget everything else. Most especially, that hurt.

And he did. He held her tight as she buckled beneath his onslaught. As she screamed her sudden release. But it wasn't enough. He pulled her to the floor and plunged to the hilt into her heat.

Rocking his hips, he drove the rhythm he knew she loved. Her hands gripped him hard, her fingers pinching and pushing to hurry him. He wasn't having it. Not until she was on the edge again. Not until she was arching uncontrollably, her hair tumbling, her skin flushed and gleaming, her cries quickening.

Only then did he let himself go again, surging into her soft, searing, sweet-as-heaven body and finding his own satisfaction. His own breath was stolen and his heart raced. He was almost dizzy with both relief and the sudden renewal of desire. He lifted his head and stared down at her beauty.

Again. Again. Again. It would *never* be enough.

He saw the shock in her eyes—the widening, then the *wonder*. Belatedly, he realised his mistake. She was confusing this passion, this addiction to mutual pleasure, for *feelings*. The depth of which he didn't have. He *couldn't*.

But he couldn't pull back, couldn't make himself let go of the melting pleasure to be found in her arms. *All* control was gone. Which meant tonight had to be the last time.

'Please, please, please…' Carrie begged him again and again and again.

Only it wasn't begging. It was *asking* for what she wanted. What she needed.

Love me. Love me. Love me.

He filled her again. He took her right to where she wanted to go. But it wasn't enough. He held her. He touched her. But it wasn't enough, even after the next orgasm shattered her and left her limp. Even when her lips were salty from the sweat dampening her face, her pretty dress was shredded and she simply couldn't move. It wasn't enough.

Even when he set about making her come apart all over again, it wasn't enough. It would *never* be enough.

CHAPTER SIXTEEN

'MASSIMO…'

He didn't reply.

'Massi—'

'Don't, Carrie.' He turned his head to look at her and this time the expression in his eyes was sombre. 'Don't.'

He'd taken her to heaven and she—wanton, reckless, desperate lover that she was—hadn't just *let* him, she'd spurred him on, breathlessly demanding he hurry. She'd been such a willing participant in her own destruction. The assumption of that woman tonight—that Massimo was only with her because of their baby—was true. *How very clever of Carrie!* Wrong.

'Don't silence me,' she said. 'Not now.'

Not when she'd finally found the confidence to speak on something so important.

He flinched. 'Carrie—'

'I want more,' she said.

She wanted it all. She didn't just want the spectacular sex and the security of his name. She wanted his *love*. And she wasn't going to get it. So she needed to end it now. Not because it wasn't going to last but because it wasn't *enough*. She'd given him everything and, if she stayed, if she let this continue as it was, there would be nothing left of herself. She'd be swallowed whole while remaining incomplete. What a fool she'd been to think she could somehow have her cake and eat it too.

'I want honesty and truth and openness,' she said. 'And that needs to start with me. So here goes.' She sucked in a breath. 'I love you, Massimo. I'm utterly in love with you.'

She knew it would destroy everything, yet it was such a relief to admit it. She was so completely, utterly and irrevocably in love with him.

'It's just sex,' Massimo answered.

His default setting was blanket denial—as with when she'd told him she was pregnant all those months ago. He didn't believe her. She knew he had trust issues—but surely he trusted her word now?

She shook her head. 'We just shared *so* much more than that. Lust, yes, absolutely. But don't you get why it was so frantic?' She stared at his frozen face, willing him to go with her on this.

'That need was love, Massimo. I opened up and let you in. That's what you wanted. That's what you took. I wanted it too.'

'It's just physical for me.' He pushed away from her. 'It was frantic because it's been a while. It's a biological urge and response. That's all.'

His words welted her heart.

'That's not true.' Her breathing quickened. 'You can't get enough.' Her chin lifted with the last of her courage. 'Same as me.'

'Because it's a *temporary* high,' he said. 'I *warned* you.' His eyes closed. 'It won't last.'

But he'd also told her that chemistry like this couldn't be contained.

'You do not get to deny or debase what that was.' Her anger surged. 'And, while I love sex *with* you, you are not *only* sex to me. I'm being as honest, as clear, as I can. Letting you see right through me to my heart. To what matters. To *all* that matters. And you're…'

Unable to say anything. Because—she realised with horror—it wasn't that he didn't *believe* her. It was because he couldn't give her the answer she so desperately wanted. Because he'd already told her and *she* was the one not listening. He'd told her not to settle for second best. Not to let herself be undervalued any more. To make a scene if necessary, not to stay silent. That she was stronger than that.

But she wasn't. She was not strong enough. Because the truth was *he* didn't want to settle for her. *He* didn't love *her.* She wasn't enough for him. She wasn't wanted by him for anything more than sex. Which meant she had to push him away. Because *he* was her paradise. And her paradise had become her prison. Her life, her heart, was now irrevocably bound with his. Because with Ana they were a tightly woven group that couldn't be separated.

But they could be loosened.

She ached to breathe freely. She was going to have to live with it somehow. And she would, because of her daughter. But she was *not* settling. She was not staying silent. Not this time. Not any more, ever again.

'You know, that night back in Auckland, you were my treat,' she said sadly. 'My indulgence just for me. No real risk. I *knew* you were leaving. I *knew* you weren't meant for me. And because of that I wasn't going to fall in love with you. That was never a threat. You weren't supposed to be a *threat.*'

Even though she'd known he was so far out of her league, she'd rolled with the *chemistry*. She'd run with the fantasy of it. Only it had all fallen apart because, when confronted with the reality of him all those months later in Fiji—when faced with the tough things, when they'd reconnected, when she'd got to know his depths—was when she'd *really* fallen.

'I didn't want to see you again. That first night was dangerous enough. That's why I never phoned. I *knew* this would happen.' Even though she'd tried to save pride and denied that it would. Now there was no pride left.

He was still frozen. This was not what he wanted to hear. Of course it wasn't.

'Carrie…'

She bowed her head. 'You don't feel the same way.'

'I can't.' He stared at her grimly. 'I don't want this, Carrie. I'm not capable—'

'You don't want *me*,' she argued, hurt by his easy excuses. 'You're not a robot, Massimo. You love Ana.'

He drew a sharp breath. 'That's different.'

'Yes, but at the same time it isn't,' she said. 'You can love when you want to. You *let* yourself love her. You let her in. I think you didn't have a choice about that, really, because it's Ana.' She breathed harder. 'But you won't let yourself love me. You won't let me in *because* it's me. One day with someone else there'll be no choice. You won't be able to say no.'

'That's not going to happen. Ever.'

He really believed he didn't want love in his life.

'You really think that you can *control* it?'

'Yes.'

'I can't stay here any more.' She climbed out of bed and pulled on the nearest pair of jeans. They were his and they fell straight off.

He stood and snatched them from her. 'Where do you think you can go right now?'

'Anywhere. I've fallen in love with you and that's not what you want. And I can't stay here to be—'

'Well, you can't run away.' His anger rose. 'Ana anchors you here. She always will. And she tethers us together. You can't just *escape* from this.'

'No, but I can *cope*,' she snapped. 'And distance from *you* is essential for me to do that. Some space. Take my passport, if you want. Take Ana's. You know I'll never leave *her*. But *we* don't have to stay together.' She glared at him. 'You can't have your cake and eat it, Massimo. *I'm* not that convenient. I'm not going to make it easy. Not this time. Not any more.'

'What more do I have to do to make you happy?' His temper shredded. 'I bought that bloody island for you.'

'I never asked you to buy me anything. You just did that because you *could*. Because it's power and control for you. I don't give a damn about islands or clothes or *things*. I care about *you*. The person you are when you let your guard down.' She gazed at him, desolation filling her so fast. 'But you shouldn't have to *try* to make me happy. You know you don't really want me to stay, and I *can't* be here with you like this. It's not fair, Massimo. You need to let me go.'

Abruptly he turned and pulled on his jeans. 'Then let's enact these changes tonight.' He now displayed nothing but business-like precision.

She watched as the war within him was lost— so quickly. He didn't want to fight for her. So she'd won. And she was *devastated*. She couldn't swallow...could hardly speak. 'I'll go to—'

'*I'll* leave,' he snapped. 'You're not going anywhere.'

'No, that's not fair.' She breathed raggedly. 'This is your home. *I* need somewhere else. I'll find somewhere to rent.' She winced. 'I'm sorry I've cost you so much.'

'Money is irrelevant.'

She hadn't meant money—not entirely. She'd meant time and resources. But now he was icy and proactive.

'We would have had separate residences eventually anyway. The other apartments are already vacant. It's no problem for me to go to mine now while you stay here with Ana. When it's my turn to spend time with her, you'll go to your personal apartment. It's only a brief walk from here. That way it's less disruptive to Ana and we don't need to duplicate all of her things. We can eventually, of course, but it will be good for her to remain in familiar surroundings initially. It's easier for Leah too.'

'That's…' Carrie swallowed. 'That's a good idea.'

But she was stunned. Not only had Massimo worked out an action plan for when they were no longer together, he'd *already done* all the preparation. Those apartments were ready *now*. Which meant he'd been mulling this for a while, whereas she'd only had a lightning strike realisation minutes ago. When she'd fully opened up, only to be shot down by him. Bitterness trickled. 'And you say I'm the one who runs away? You've got your escape plan hatched perfectly.'

He shot her a glance. 'It was only a matter of time.'

Yet he was the one who'd insisted on them living together in the first place. He'd spent time with her, making her laugh, making her feel good, making her fall for him. Until she'd got too close. He was so cruel.

'Self-fulfilling prophecies, don't you think?' Disappointment flooded her. And anger. So much anger. 'You *expected* me to end it. You *made* me want to. Because you're too cowardly to envisage an alternative altogether. You can't possibly believe that this could have lasted. You refused to *ever* seriously entertain the idea.'

His face stiffened. 'Actually, you're wrong. I did wonder if this could last longer. But that would only be possible if it remained as it was.'

As some convenient arrangement.

'So it's my fault for speaking up? For asking for more? For wanting to name what's *really* between us?'

It was the one thing he'd encouraged her to do.

Devastated, she watched him throw a few things into a carry-all. His automatic movements just proved his lack of care. Yet, if she hadn't said anything, he would have been happy to keep sleeping with her. He'd been *using* her.

Silence would have kept this easy. Silence would have betrayed her. She couldn't stay silent any more.

'I can't give you *everything*.' Her voice rose. 'Why should I give and give when you don't want it all from me? When you don't want to give *me* everything in return?' She caught the sudden look of fury from him. 'I'm not talking about tangibles, Massimo. I'm talking about more precious things—time, consideration, to be thought of *first*. To be your number one...'

That was all she wanted. To be someone's number one. And, while the love he showed for Ana redeemed him, it ripped her heart into pieces. Because it showed how he could love. Just not her.

'Why should I hurt myself wishing that one day you might? The convenience of me was a plus, but it doesn't really matter. I know you'll be a good father for Ana. But you don't have to be a good husband for me. Not any more. You like sex? You're free to get it from someone else. My blessings.'

He threw her look of such fury, she actually stepped back.

'You ask for too much!' He growled.

'You told me I should say how I felt. Or didn't you think I'd apply that advice directly to you?'

'But because you didn't get the answer you wanted, you just want to run away.'

'From you, yes.'

'Good. Because I *cannot* be the man you want me to be. I am *not* the man you think you love.'

What did he even mean by that? 'Of course you are,' she said. And for one last, devastating time she was compelled to admit the truth. 'I love you, Massimo. *All* of you. Flaws and all. *Fears* and all.'

But he didn't even see her any more. He just scooped up the bag and stalked out of the apartment.

Carrie stared after him, shattered. She'd just offered him everything. But it wasn't enough. *She* wasn't enough.

CHAPTER SEVENTEEN

MASSIMO SWALLOWED A painkiller and winced. He hadn't had a sore throat like this in years. The childhood complaint had come back to haunt him when he needed it least.

Week two of the new arrangement.

He'd known it wouldn't last. He'd known she would leave. When she didn't get what she wanted, when she was overwhelmed, she tried to escape. But *he* was the one who'd gone. *He'd* clawed back his control and not allowed emotion to overrule reason. He'd been strong enough to do what was sensible. Only it hadn't really been strength. It had been self-preservation. He'd had to get out of there before the tumultuous emotion toppled his equilibrium entirely. Control? Not so much.

He missed Ana unbearably. But Leah sent him through photos and little movies on the days he was apart from her.

He missed Carrie. Awfully. So awfully, he

couldn't stand to think of her. Yet he couldn't stop. Why hadn't it been enough that he'd supported her when she'd dealt with those people at the fund-raiser? He'd been in her corner. He'd reached out to her. He'd wanted her to do what she wanted. And he'd wanted to make her feel good. Why couldn't that have been enough? Why had she then wanted to *name* what she felt? Why had she asked him for more?

Promises. Declarations. They meant nothing. Nothing could be that *certain* or that *intense*. Now, he'd not got far enough away. The fool in him wanted to go back, to try to seduce her back into that convenient marriage. He could smooth everything over and get that easy life back. But even if he succeeded it would only end the same way. Because, while they might work on that superficial level for a while, it wouldn't be long before the fissures ripped open again. Before she wanted more than he could give. And, if they ignored that, resentment would set in. Everything would rot. So it was better to finish it now before the damage became too great. They could be distant but civil, and co-parent Ana.

This way he'd not hurt her *too* much. Because what she'd said, that declaration, wasn't true. It was the confusion he'd feared would happen because of her inexperience. She only *thought* she was in love with him. She barely knew him.

But she was constantly stuck in his head. He thought of her the instant he woke and all through the day. Of course, he'd already spent all night dreaming of her. The only time he had any respite was when he forced his concentration upon mundane concerns. That quickly grew exhausting. *Carrie* was all-consuming.

It was everything he'd never wanted. He was his father—allowing his life to be ruined by feelings for a woman. His anger turned to the man who'd taught him everything so damned badly. Nolan Wells had blamed Massimo for the loss of the love of his life and had been glad when bitter facts had released him from the duty he'd never wanted. Massimo's throat really hurt now, reminding him of that surgery. The horror immediately after when his father had walked out and left him alone as he'd literally vomited blood.

'Are you going to tell him about Ana?'

He'd been appalled by Carrie's question. He wanted Ana to have what he hadn't had—protection and the security of knowing who her family was. Never to be abandoned by a parent—blood or not. As Carrie had said then, why go for repeated rejection?

Nolan Wells wouldn't accept Ana as his grandchild. He wouldn't even be interested. But somehow, two weeks after walking out on Carrie, Massimo found himself on a flight north. And he found his mother's widower on the local golf course. He'd known he would—Nolan had always loved golf.

'Massimo.' The man straightened and glanced at his watch. 'This is a surprise.'

'I wanted to invite you to Sydney to meet someone,' Massimo said. 'If you're interested.'

'Who's that?'

'Ana. My daughter.'

Nolan angled his head to look at the photo Massimo had unlocked on his phone.

Ana in her cot, looking straight up at the camera. Looking straight-up adorable.

Nolan's expression stayed impassive. 'She has your mother's eyes.'

The ones Nolan couldn't bear to look at. The ones that reminded him both of happiness and the heartbreak of betrayal.

'Does that mean you don't want to meet her?' Massimo asked.

'I don't see the point, do you?' Nolan asked. 'She's not my granddaughter.'

Massimo shouldn't have been surprised or hurt.

But he felt the surge of rage. 'You really think that?' he challenged him.

Why hadn't Nolan found the strength—the love—to forgive her?

Your poor father. So devastated. That was what everyone had said when he'd been a child—the nanny and the headmaster of the boarding school. But it wasn't true.

'You didn't love my mother at all.' Massimo shook his head.

'I loved her utterly,' Nolan said. 'But she betrayed me.'

'Why had she needed to?' Massimo asked unevenly.

'We agreed to leave it to fate,' Nolan said stiffly. 'If it was meant to happen, it would have.'

'So she knew you wouldn't accept a child that you didn't believe was your own. She knew you wouldn't compromise.'

'Why would I want to wreck my life looking after someone else's brat?' Nolan shook his head. 'As it was, she changed. She wasn't there when I wanted her.'

Because it had all been about *him*. What he'd wanted—at his convenience.

Massimo turned and walked away before his rage exploded. What he'd been taught to believe had been a deep and desperate love that had lasted beyond even death hadn't actually been love at all. It had been selfish and controlling and it sure wasn't healthy.

And his father had *used* his grief. It had enabled him to do as he wanted. Everything he'd not wanted to deal with he'd allowed others to take on—such as his son. Even when he'd believed Massimo was his own blood, he'd not wanted to be bothered. There was no *love* in that. There was only self-indulgence.

And, if he'd really loved Massimo's mother, why hadn't he got past the initial hurt of discovering the truth about Massimo? Why hadn't he tried to understand it? Wouldn't he have found the strength to forgive her? Wouldn't he have had the insight to understand why she'd done what she had? Wouldn't he have loved her son regardless? Because her son was the one part of her that lived on.

Why had he taken it out on Massimo? Why had he not even given him a chance? Because Nolan hadn't wanted Massimo from the beginning and it had been a completely convenient escape from him. Massimo's feelings for Ana crystallised everything. Because Ana was *Carrie's* child, and Massimo would do anything to protect her, even if biology proved she wasn't his. Which meant Nolan hadn't cared for Massimo's mother the way Massimo cared for Carrie.

And Nolan hadn't been devastated. Massimo remembered the golf trips, the work travel… His father had just wanted to escape all emotional *responsibility* and he'd used grief, then betrayal, as his excuses. He'd been liberated to live the life he wanted. He wasn't just selfish. He was incapable of love.

The lie that Massimo had been fed was about what love was at all.

Did Massimo want that freedom to do whatever he wanted? He'd had it—all his adult life he'd had it. But where was the woman to tease, the child to snatch up and cuddle? Where was the laughter, the joy in sharing those moments? In sharing them with *Carrie*.

When Massimo returned to his office a large yellow envelope stood out amongst the mail on his desk.

Private and confidential.

The sender stamp showed it was from the lawyer. He'd need to contact the guy and talk about how they could safely progress Carrie's residency status. But for now Massimo ripped the edge and tipped the envelope up. Several official documents scattered out. Their wedding certificate. Ana's birth certificate. The results of the DNA test. A glance at each showed what he already knew. Carrie was his wife. Ana was named for Sereana. And Ana was his daughter. Mere pieces of paper that were meaningless. Only serving to smooth the process of keeping Carrie in the country.

But he stared at the letter confirming his paternity. No, it wouldn't have mattered what that damned DNA test showed. Ana was Carrie's child and as such she was precious to him. But there was more than that. He'd had only a week with her in Fiji, but Massimo *knew* Ana, and he adored her. He loved the snuffling noises she made in her sleep…the way she made a small fist, like a prize fighter, the softness of her hair, her unutterably sweet smile.

Massimo wanted to be there when she took her first steps and said her first words. He wanted her to turn to him when she was tearful. He wanted to make her laugh. He didn't want to miss a thing and he couldn't wait to see how she grew as a person. He wanted to be right alongside her—to encourage, guide and just love. He loved *her*— Carrie's child—as who she was, as she was, as she would be. He couldn't love her more and there was nothing she could do to make him love her less. What he felt was infinite, yet utterly complete, and he had no problem admitting any of that.

That was love, wasn't it? Unconditional, unending, freely given and, now he'd realised it, utterly liberating. It was the kind of love *he'd* never been given.

Maybe his mother would have done, but she'd died before she could. His father—incapable. But, in seeing the destructive ashes of his parents' relationship, Massimo had learned to keep people distant and intimacy frankly transactional. It had been safer to stay alone.

Carrie was the only person ever to tell him she loved him and he hadn't believed her. He'd been too stunned. Too scared. Afraid that, once she really knew him, she'd want to leave him. Everyone else had, right? He'd thought he didn't have whatever it was he needed to keep people close—that he was missing something. He realised now that he wasn't. All that was wrong with him was fear. Because Carrie had offered him the one thing he'd been too afraid to admit he'd ever want.

I love you, Massimo. All *of you. Flaws and all.* Fears *and all.*

He'd taken only what had felt safe. Had limited them to sex. But he'd been unable to resist stealing more. The marriage that had been for convenience was so much more. He'd *wanted* to marry her. He just hadn't wanted to admit it. There were so many things about his feelings for Carrie that he hadn't wanted to admit.

He pulled out his phone and looked again at the photo his assistant had released to the media. They were on the beach just after the wedding. Carrie held Ana in her arms as she laughed up at him. It was a picture so perfect, it couldn't possibly be real. It couldn't possibly last.

Yet it was real. He'd not just seen it, he'd lived it. And as for lasting? He'd not had faith in her but he'd had even less in himself. He'd not believed anyone could love him for long because no one ever had.

Sometimes faith was believing in something unseen. Sometimes it was believing in something that hadn't yet happened—the faith was believing that it *would.* Massimo's faith—his trust—had long been in the inevitable *failure* of relationships. Ultimately in abandonment. People lied, they died or they left. The love he'd been shown was destructive and it hadn't lasted. But what he'd been taught was love hadn't been at all. Love was so much more and so much *easier*. Especially when you just gave in—accepting it, *admitting* it.

Why had he feared a future with Carrie? Feared growing old alongside her, sharing in the joy of raising Ana and the possible marvel of giving her a sibling—one they'd adore just as much, just as easily? Why had he allowed the hurts of so long ago—of other people—scar and influence him? He'd been blind to his real choices, the real likelihoods. He'd been blind to what was *real* faith, trust and love.

He paced impatiently. He wasn't going use past hurt to hide from future hope now. Carrie had run away from what hurt her, but she still had hope. She was an optimist, and she was brave, and she'd *tried* with him. She'd shown such courage in telling him her feelings. he advice he'd given her, he needed to take himself. To let her know how afraid he was, what a damned fool he'd been, what he really felt. He'd wanted to provide security and protection for Ana because *he'd* longed for security and protection. Carrie wanted Ana to be put first—for their daughter to know she was the priority. Because Carrie never had been.

Until now. Now she was utterly, and always would be, *his* priority. He just had to prove it to her.

CHAPTER EIGHTEEN

ON THE NIGHTS when Massimo had his time with Ana, Carrie left the apartment extra early so there was no chance of her departure overlapping with his arrival. Massimo would never be late for his daughter. Knowing how much he cared for Ana was both balm and bitter poison. She had to protect the remnants of her crushed heart, needing time and space for healing to begin. Though it was almost three weeks since he'd left and it felt like any healing had hardly started.

But she forced her focus forward. She was doing it for Ana. Not just surviving, thriving. It was important that Ana see her mother valuing *herself*. Even if she didn't get all she yearned for, it was better than accepting less. Massimo had done so much for her, but in truth only because he'd had to, not because he'd wanted to. She wouldn't have seen him again if it hadn't been for Ana. The chemistry still between them wasn't enough. And it wasn't enough for her to sneak under his guard and be near to him because of that. He needed to *let* her in—to do more than allow her in his life, but actually *want* her in his life in that way.

She'd desperately wanted him to open up and admit that she was the one that he would give up almost anything to be with. Only he hadn't. She'd gambled, asked and lost. But she'd spoken up. And that was the real start.

So the twice-weekly night away from Ana was the time to work on her future. She couldn't dwell on her memories of Massimo. Couldn't reflect on the way he cradled Ana with such tender care or on the love that shone in his eyes as he looked at her. She loved that he loved their child but was so hurt that he didn't love *her*.

And so much of what he'd said was right. She couldn't escape. Couldn't run away. She had to deal with her reality, as hard as it was. And she could. Because she'd found dignity in having spoken her truth. Even though it hadn't worked out the way she'd wanted it to, she'd done it.

She'd registered with an agency and had been contracted for a few hours a week to supplement what she could still do for Sereana. So she had something outside herself and her own heartache to focus on. She enjoyed it. She was good at it, and she had plans to develop her sports event-scheduling app.

It was necessary for her self-worth and an independent future. Sure, she wasn't going to need the money, but she needed the satisfaction and purpose. She was good at arranging, at being the sounding board for decisions, for taking away the tasks that were a waste of other people's time. Not because their time was more precious than hers but, because *she* was skilled, it took her less time. She could do the detail that others couldn't see.

Her apartment was barely three minutes' walk. It was plush but impersonal. She'd not bothered to make it her own. It was too big for the two nights a week she stayed, but that was Massimo—providing far too much of some things while withholding the thing she wanted most. Himself.

She didn't know where he stayed the five nights she was alone with Ana. It wasn't at this apartment. It wasn't her business. But she was all ache. In weak moments she regretted her stand. If she'd stayed silent she could still have been with him now, except it would've been a slow torture. He didn't love her and it would have ended eventually. Better to have taken control of it herself. To have stood up for herself.

Today, the door man came over as soon as he saw her. 'I'm sorry, Carrie.' He addressed her informally, as she'd asked him to a couple of weeks ago. 'The apartment is having work done and it's taken longer than anticipated. You can't stay here tonight. Massimo has left this for you, and I have a taxi waiting.'

'Oh?' Frowning, she took the envelope from him.

She opened it as the doorman gave the taxi driver the address. Inside was a key card and a typed note listing a room number. Nothing personal, just the problem solved in true money-fixes-all style. Doubtless there'd be some new outfit there for her to wear tomorrow. Massimo always thought of everything. She drew a deep breath. Okay. She'd have the night at a hotel. Maybe she'd drink her way through the entire damned mini-bar and order everything on the menu.

Only he'd done the 'everything on the menu' thing for her once already, and she wasn't in the least hungry. As soon as she got to the hotel she went straight to the lift. It soared to the top floor. Opening the door, she took another deep breath.

It wasn't just a room, it was an entire suite, and the view across the city…

She glimpsed it only briefly because then she noticed the table—it was smothered in dishes. Did she have the wrong room? She'd phone Reception, because there'd clearly been a mistake. But, before she could, someone knocked at the door. Probably a porter come to say she had the wrong key card. So she opened the door without checking the peephole.

Instant regret. Instant freeze.

Massimo Donati-Wells. Tall, dark and damning her wretched heart to hell in one swift second. It had been almost three weeks since he'd walked out. Since they'd shared breathing space. Since *everything*. Now he was at her door in a sharply tailored suit, but it was the stormy look in his eyes that cut her to ribbons.

'You don't have to let me in if you don't want to,' he said unevenly.

Her legs lacked strength. All of her lacked strength. As if she could say no to him!

'Carrie.'

His step forward gave her enough impetus to step back. She couldn't bear his touch. She was nowhere near over him. She needed space or she would give him everything. She couldn't do that.

Massimo stepped inside and closed the door behind him. Another swift glance into her distraught face sent his heart sprinting. Had he made a massive mistake?

'You're supposed to be with Ana,' she said. 'Is something wrong?'

'No,' he reassured her. 'Leah's with her. She's safe and well. This is…' He dragged in a breath.

He could hardly think for the relief of seeing her again. For the anxiety—pending the outcome of this meeting. He had to fight the urge to pull her into his arms and kiss her as if his life depended on it. Which, frankly, it did.

'What?' She bit her lip worriedly. 'Is there anything wrong with the apartment, or is this just part of some plan?'

Yeah, his plan was falling apart already.

'I had to go away for work.' He cleared his throat. 'Actually, I had to make it impossible to come and see you.'

'Because I'm so terrifying?' Her face was pale.

It took everything not to reach for her. But she deserved more than that. She deserved the words, the truth, first.

'I went and saw my father.'

Her eyes dilated. 'You what?'

'I asked if he wanted to meet Ana. It didn't go

well.' He sighed. This wasn't working out anything like how he'd planned, and he couldn't explain it easily. 'I didn't want to be like him. I didn't ever want to love someone so much that losing them would be that devastating. But that's not what's happened. Really, he used the loss of my mother as an excuse to live selfishly. He wouldn't compromise for her. Or for me. He didn't *love* either of us.

'What I thought was love…?' He shook his head. He wasn't making sense. She wasn't understanding him. She was just staring at him.

'I thought it was my fault,' he muttered helplessly. 'That Mum wanting me so much led to her infidelity and then to her death. He couldn't bear to look at me. He didn't want me. I thought it was something in *me*.' He rolled his shoulders. 'And I guess I shut down. I thought I had it all under control so I wouldn't be like him. I wouldn't be hurt. Relationships were recreational. Just a good time, right?'

He stared into her eyes. 'Sex was all I gave. All I wanted to give. Until you.'

Carrie couldn't let hope unfurl. She glanced around the suite to avoid looking in his eyes. The flowers in the vases were reminiscent of the arrangements in Fiji. On the table she saw coconut rice, spiced fish, sweet pineapple. The dishes had been deliberately chosen—things she liked. He wanted to please her.

'I want to give you everything,' he said quietly.

She began to tremble.

'I miss Ana,' he added. 'I miss *you*. And I want you to have all of me. If you want.'

She half-flinched, half-held herself back. But he took a step towards her.

'I'm *not* like him. You were right, I'm just me. Carrie, I've been hurt. I'm a bit damaged. I have some work to do and I am screwing this up. But I am here for you, and I will *always* be here for you because, married or not, I want *you*. Only you. Always you, and I want to be *with* you—in everything, every day. And it wouldn't matter if I was or wasn't Ana's father. I would still love her because she is herself and she is wonderful and she is also *yours*. She is a vital, precious part of you, and I adore *you*. *You* are who I want with me in this. With me in everything.'

She couldn't move or speak or even start to believe the wonderful, magical things he was saying. The things she wanted so very much. Now he was so close, she could feel his heat and the soft, warm breath of his whisper.

'I'm so sorry, Carrie.' His murmur hurt. 'I

wasn't honest. Not with myself or you, and I hurt you a lot.'

But she shook her head. 'I'm not the woman anyone expects you to be with.'

'In what way?'

'I'm not…'

He waited.

'You're successful.' She swallowed. 'And handsome. And everything. Just everything.'

'And the one woman in the world I can't resist is you.'

'That's just sex. Chemistry.'

'Turning my cowardice on me, Carrie? You know damn well it isn't.' He grabbed her waist and pulled her flush against him. 'You can't deny what it really is. You're too warm, too loyal, too brave. *I'm* the coward here. I wanted to resist, Carrie. *I* was too scared to understand what love even is, let alone accept it. But you? You're a fighter. You fought for Ana. You fought for me. I want to fight for *us*.'

She couldn't let herself believe him. She *couldn't*. She pushed on his chest. 'But you'll get bored. Eventually you'll want someone else.'

He stilled, his expression turning solemn, but he didn't release her. 'I am willing to spend the rest of my life working on your self-esteem, Carrie. Because it breaks my heart that you can't believe that *you're enough* for me.'

She felt hot and cold and horrible, and tears filled her eyes because that was her fear uttered aloud.

'You are, sweetheart.' He cupped her face in his hand. 'You always have been. Always will be. Enough. Just as you are. Funny and smart and generous and *so* genuine.'

His green eyes gleamed with strength and surety. 'I thought I had everything, Carrie. Every success, right? But these last weeks have proved I had nothing of real value.' His hands were so gentle on her now, stroking the side of her neck in that way she simply couldn't resist. 'I didn't think I could ever emotionally commit. Or would ever want to. I didn't want to invest because I didn't want to lose. I couldn't bear it if you abandoned me. But I have to offer you all I can. I'm yours, always yours, if you want me. I want everything with you.'

'But if it weren't for Ana…' she whispered.

'I would have found you in Fiji anyway,' he whispered back, the most gorgeously rueful smile creasing the corners of his eyes. 'Why couldn't I resist investigating investment opportunities on a Pacific paradise? I couldn't get you out of my head. I left you my number. I *wanted* you to contact me,' he said. 'To ask. But you didn't. And I didn't either. I didn't want to accept how much of an impact you had on me. But suddenly there I am, in Fiji. Glancing around in case I spotted you. It was my *third* trip, Carrie.'

'Third?' Her heart skidded.

'It was so easy that night in Auckland. Intense but easy. I didn't want to let you go home alone after dinner but I thought it was for the best. Something in me was scared even then. Subconsciously I knew you were special. And then you came back to me at the marina and it was magic.' His smile was twisted with sadness and hope. 'Come back to me again, Carrie. Come back… but this time stay for always.'

His insistence, his touch, the emotion shining in his eyes…

'Okay.' She collapsed against him.

'Will you ever believe how much I love you?' he murmured between kisses that jump-started everything. 'How much I want you? *Nothing* matters more than having you in my life.'

She closed her eyes, sure she was dreaming. 'Promise?'

'Always, and again and again. I'll tell you. I'll show you. I'll love you and I'll never leave you.

You're *my* number one, Carrie, and I want you and Ana in the centre of my life. I want you to stay there.'

'Yes, please.' Now her tears fell. Now her body shook. Now she knew. 'Don't let me go.'

'Never.'

They moved together—magic, intense—tumbling to the floor in hot, fast, sweet desperation. Feeling him tremble at the lightest touch, she realised that, like him, she needed security. She'd secretly longed not for someone who would just ask her to stay, but someone who'd really see her, value her and *want* her right there with him. Here he was. Her anchor. Her everything. And he was so wonderful.

'I love you, Massimo,' she sobbed.

With every piece of her she loved him—hard—until she felt emotion tear him apart in a release more passionate, more intense, than any they'd shared before. They kissed and touched, coming together hotly and fiercely until they could barely breathe. They lay tangled for a long, long while.

'I think we should go back to the island soon,' he murmured contentedly. 'We need more of a honeymoon.'

'Yes, please.' She laced her fingers through his. 'But do you think we can go home to Ana now?'

Her arms ached for their daughter. For them to start anew *together*—their whole little family. She saw the softening in his eyes. The understanding. The *love*. He sat up and scrambled for their clothes so fast, she laughed.

'I can't wait to see her,' he admitted with a goofy smile. 'And I'm *never* sleeping apart from you again.'

'Just like that?' she teased.

He held out his hand to help her to her feet. 'Just like that.'

EPILOGUE

Three years later

MASSIMO STRETCHED LANGUOROUSLY, appreciating the warmth invading his body. It was more than the sun penetrating his skin, it was love steam-cleaning his soul. He watched Carrie the gorgeous, clad in a bikini and some floaty fabric, scoop up their daughter and for a second he wondered if his heart might actually burst.

But then his daughter giggled. Ana had been yawning for the last ten minutes as she too was tired from swimming in the clear water with him these last two hours. Leah stepped forward from where she'd been reading to take her to the nursery, leaving Massimo and Carrie alone in the secluded, shady nook on their private beach.

Massimo loved his life. He especially loved afternoon nap time. He knew this level of contentment was rare. Nowadays he felt rested in a way he'd neither experienced, nor even imagined possible, only a few years ago. And his happy heart beat faster as Carrie strolled towards where he lay sprawled back on the warm sand, mirth sparkling in her eyes.

'Massimo Donati-Wells,' she addressed him with mock civility. 'Are you lazing on the beach doing *nothing*?'

'Not doing nothing,' he replied extremely lazily, yet with a huskiness that betrayed the depths of his emotions. 'I'm plotting.'

'Nefarious takeover plans? Corporate raiding? Some high-profile merger?' Even as she teased there was a softness in her expression.

'Definitely a merger. There's a distinct possibility of a takeover as well.'

The shimmer in her eyes brightened.

He sat up to take her hand, then tugged on it as he lay back again. He didn't have to tug hard—she tumbled to the sand beside him. It was a slow, laughing tumble that she'd totally expected. Because, no, it wasn't the first time he'd made that move. He pushed back the floaty covering so he could touch her. His need to feel her skin against his was almost a torture.

'How is it possible that you're seven months' pregnant?' he whispered in wonder. He knew her and yet she was still such a wondrous mystery to him.

Her shoulders lifted and even she shook her head in bemusement. 'It's just the way I seem to carry them.'

There were small tell-tale signs that did betray her to those closely observant. And right now Massimo was very, very close and very, very observant. He reverentially explored each sign—kissing along that softer line of her jaw, smoothing his palms over her radiant skin, carefully pushing aside the small stretchy bikini so he could ever so gently press his teeth into the deeper blush of her nipples. The curve to her belly, the one that had always been there, wasn't much bigger than usual yet it was little more than two months until her due date.

'You're incredible,' he muttered.

Enchanting. Bewitching. Loving. Generous. Funny. Sharp.

She was so many wonderful things and he was about to lazily make love to his wife for as long as possible. Although in truth it wasn't going to be *that* long, because she felled him. The attraction burned even hotter than in those heady days when they'd first married, when they'd first realised and admitted their love.

But, while there was peace in being with her right in this present moment, there was the paradox of desperation as well. Desire pushed him to move faster even when he wanted to take all the time there was in existence to simply savour this moment. *Every* moment.

Carrie rubbed the backs of her fingers along Massimo's stubbly jawline. She loved him most like this—a little tired, a lot relaxed, with all the love shining from his eyes.

Vulnerable together. Content together. No distraction. No distance. Nothing *but* them. Their family and friends were nearby and they would dine and laugh together later. But this moment? This was theirs alone.

Their son was due soon and Carrie couldn't wait to meet him. Massimo had already started talking about another child after him. He, who'd once been so determined not to have children at *all*, now wanted a large family. And he wanted to share in all the experiences life could offer. He'd pushed back on the hours he worked, striving to better balance their world. He supported her endeavours at work—becoming *her* champion, the supporter she'd lacked for so long. It wasn't perfect, of course. But in that imperfect way, with mistakes and laughter, it absolutely was.

They spent long stretches of time in Fiji. Eventually school terms or work schedules might limit their time there for a while, but she was at peace with that. Because she understood that his love for her knew no limits. Just as her love for him was profoundly complete. Paradise, she'd discovered, wasn't a place. Nor was it an escape. It was simply being with *him*—in the time and space they shared.

Here. Now. Together.

* * * * *